Rex Stout, the creator of Indiana, in 1886, the six Lucetta Todhunter Stout, both Quakers. Shortly after his birth the family moved to Wakarusa, Kansas. He was educated in a country school, but by the age of nine he was recognized throughout the state as a prodigy in arithmetic. Mr. Stout briefly attended the University of Kansas, but he left to enlist in the Navy and spent the next two years as a warrant officer on board President Theodore Roosevelt's yacht. When he left the Navy in 1908, Rex Stout began to write freelance articles and worked as a sightseeing guide and an itinerant book-keeper. Later he devised and implemented a school banking system which was installed in four hundred cities and towns throughout the country. In 1927 Mr. Stout retired from the world of finance and, with the proceeds of his banking scheme, left for Paris to write serious fiction. He wrote three novels that received favorable reviews before turning to detective fiction. His first Nero Wolfe novel, *Fer-de-Lance*, appeared in 1934. It was followed by many others, among them, *Too Many Cooks, The Silent Speaker, If Death Ever Slept, The Doorbell Rang*, and *Please Pass the Guilt*, which established Nero Wolfe as a leading character

Gardner's famous protagonist, P
War II Rex Stout waged a person
as chairman of the War Writers' B
of the radio program "Speaking
several national committees. Afte
tention to mobilizing public opini
of thermonuclear devices, was a
thors' Guild, and resumed writing
Stout died in 1975 at the age of e
his death he published his seven
tery, *A Family Affair*. Ten years
Wolfe mystery was discovered an
Three.

The Rex Stout Library

REX STOUT

Three Witnesses

Introduction
by Susan Conant

BANTAM BOOKS
NEW YORK • TORONTO • LONDON • SYDNEY • AUCKLAND

A NERO WOLFE
MYSTERY

This edition contains the complete text
of the original hardcover edition.
NOT ONE WORD HAS BEEN OMITTED

THREE WITNESSES

Bantam Crime Line Book / published by arrangement
with Viking Penguin

PUBLISHING HISTORY
Viking edition published March 1956
Bantam edition / July 1957
Bantam reissue edition / October 1994

CRIME LINE and the portrayal of a boxed "cl" are trademarks of Bantam
Books, a division of Random House, Inc.

ISBN 0-553-24959-2

Published simultaneously in the United States and Canada

Bantam Books are published by Bantam Books, a division of Random House,
Inc. Its trademark, consisting of the words "Bantam Books" and the portrayal
of a rooster, is Registered in U.S. Patent and Trademark Office and in other
countries. Marca Registrada. Bantam Books, 1540 Broadway, New York, New
York 10036.

Introduction

When I was asked to introduce the novellas in this collection, I felt wary of the ominously titled "Die Like a Dog," which I had always imagined to be yet another better-left-unread mystery in which my favorite character, probably a German shepherd, would rapidly and gruesomely perish in some misguided foreshadowing of the so-called real murder. To reassure myself on the crucial quadrupedal point, I read the third of these novellas first. Delighted to discover that I could recommend it to even the most tender-hearted dog lover, I turned to the beginning of *Three Witnesses* only to find myself assailed by self-doubt. In every Rex Stout I had ever read, Archie Goodwin had ably performed the introductions with no help from me. I was thus relieved to discover that, despite their doglessness, the first two novellas in *Three Witnesses* required a few introductory remarks that I was, after all, qualified to make.

"The Next Witness" and "When a Man Murders . . ." may unintentionally mystify the reader raised in the era of telephonic electronics, digit dialing, and workshops in model mugging. Back in the old days, young reader, answering machines had not yet been invented, telephone exchanges bore evocative names like Rhinelander and Gramercy, and the women who operated switchboards were quaintly known as "girls." In those days, too, a lady who picked up a cigarette thereby compelled the nearest gentleman to offer her a light rather than a lecture on the hazards of second-hand smoke or a query about nicotine patches. I must also inform the young reader that although most of the "females" and "girls" in the world of Nero Wolfe are manipulative, neurotic, mendacious, or vacuous, Rex Stout was not actually scheming to do them in by encouraging them to smoke. As for the method of dealing with "hysterical" women that Archie employs in "When a Man Murders . . . ," I can say only that if Archie tried anything like that today, mystery fiction would lose one of its most engaging narrators.

How, then, does Rex Stout continue to enchant readers of both sexes and all political persuasions? In part by treating men and women alike as objects of critical scrutiny. More important, however, Stout simultaneously confers on the reader—any reader, male or female—so flattering a sense of membership in the vivid quasi family of Wolfe's ménage that the honored adoptee eagerly overlooks, forgives, or treasures the characteristics that define and preserve that orderly universe: Wolfe's misogyny, Archie's women-as-objects chauvinism, even Stout's formulaic plots.

These three witness-centered novellas offer three radically different perspectives on the center of that universe. In "The Next Witness," the agoraphobic, gynephobic Wolfe endures the discomfort of leaving home and suffers the intolerable sensation of finding himself seated next to a "perfumed woman." In contrast, "When a Man Murders . . ." presents the Nero Wolfe most characteristic of the series, the at-home Wolfe who retains his distance from the human specimens that appear before him.

Except in one respect, "Die Like a Dog" is also stock Stout. A murder occurs. So what? The mystery might have been written to illustrate the maxim that nobody cares about the corpse and to refute the theory that the puzzle element accounts for the genre's appeal. The exception is the charming Labrador retriever variously called Jet, Bootsy, and—tellingly, I think—Nero, perhaps the most fleshed-out nonseries character Stout ever created and a dog relegated to none of mystery's hackneyed canine roles. Not the not-quite-victim I had expected, neither is this dog a transparently human character in canine guise. In mystery after mystery, the dog is no character at all but is what psychoanalysts might call a "part object," a nose that sniffs or jaws that menace; or an apparently lifeless possession, a sort of fuzzy umbrella meant to suggest the owner's personality. Ever since "Silver Blaze" dogs have been doing nothing in the night; but in subsequent mysteries countless dogs have done nothing in the daytime, either, thereby creating no incidents, curious or otherwise. Rather, they have sat around like pieces of furniture, perhaps periodically wagging their tails as woofy cuckoo clocks. As objects of fear, dogs have at least come to life, but from the hound of the Baskervilles on, these supposedly menacing creatures have rebelliously endeared themselves to the readers they were supposed to frighten. The hound, for example, is certainly one of Doyle's most popular creations, and Baskerville remains a name lovingly bestowed on gigantic dogs.

Jet, however, is a canine witness portrayed with a

dog lover's enthusiasm and a dog fancier's accuracy. An unmistakably real dog, this rain-loving, hat-fetching creature is equally recognizable as a Labrador retriever, probably a Labrador drawn from life, perhaps even one of Stout's own, as Reed Maroc, Rex Stout's grandson, recently suggested to me. In any case, Stout knew the breed, and Nero Wolfe knows his dogs. In discussing the skull of the Labrador retriever, Wolfe almost quotes the official standard: "wide, giving brain room." Is Wolfe correct in asserting that the Labrador's skull is the widest in dogdom? Perhaps not. But hyperbolic breed loyalty is an absolute mark of the true fancier. With regard to Wolfe's claims about the relative antiquity of the basenji and the Afghan hound, the 1954 edition of the American Kennel Club's *Complete Dog Book* indicates that his was an informed, if arguable, opinion. Furthermore, it is Wolfe's ability to interpret the testimony of the canine witness that really solves the mystery.

Better yet, the dog—Jet, Bootsy, Nero—permits a rare glimpse of an emotional Nero Wolfe and of the boy he once was. Beneath the considerable flesh of the misanthropic gourmand beats the youthful heart of a dog lover, and in the agile and gregarious dog Nero beats the nonneurotic and cholesterol-free heart of the young Wolfe himself. *Nero*, the Italian for "black," the man and the dog, descendant of the wolf, Wolfe and not Wolfe, dog lover, dog fancier. It is thus my pleasure to introduce the great black dog himself: Nero Wolfe.

—Susan Conant

Contents

Three Witnesses

The
Next Witness

I

I had had previous contacts with Assistant District Attorney Irving Mandelbaum, but had never seen him perform in a courtroom. That morning, watching him at the chore of trying to persuade a jury to clamp it on Leonard Ashe for the murder of Marie Willis, I thought he was pretty good and might be better when he had warmed up. A little plump and a little short, bald in front and big-eared, he wasn't impressive to look at, but he was businesslike and self-assured without being cocky, and he had a neat trick of pausing for a moment to look at the jury as if he half expected one of them to offer a helpful suggestion. When he pulled it, not too often, his back was turned to the judge and the defense counsel, so they couldn't see his face, but I could, from where I sat in the audience.

It was the third day of the trial, and he had called his fifth witness, a scared-looking little guy with a pushed-in nose who gave his name, Clyde Bagby, took the oath, sat down, and fixed his scared brown eyes on Mandelbaum as if he had abandoned hope.

Mandelbaum's tone was reassuring. "What is your business, Mr. Bagby?"

The witness swallowed. "I'm the president of Bagby Answers Ink."

"By 'Ink' you mean 'Incorporated'?"

"Yes, sir."

"Do you own the business?"

"I own half the stock that's been issued, and my wife owns the other half."

"How long have you been operating that business?"

"Five years now—nearly five and a half."

"And what is the business? Please tell the jury about it."

Bagby's eyes went left for a quick, nervous glance at the jury box but came right back to the prosecutor. "It's a telephone-answering business, that's all. You know what that is."

"Yes, but some members of the jury may not be familiar with the operation. Please describe it."

The witness licked his lips. "Well, you're a person or a firm or an organization and you have a phone, but you're not always there and you want to know about calls that come in your absence. So you go to a tele-phone-answering service. There are several dozen of them in New York, some of them spread all over town with neighborhood offices, big operations. My own op-eration, Bagby Answers Ink, it's not so big because I specialize in serving individuals, houses and apart-ments, instead of firms or organizations. I've got offices in four different exchange districts—Gramercy, Plaza, Trafalgar, and Rhinelander. I can't work it from one central office because—"

"Excuse me, Mr. Bagby, but we won't go into tech-nical problems. Is one of your offices at six-eighteen East Sixty-ninth Street, Manhattan?"

"Yes, sir."

"Describe the operation at that address."

"Well, that's my newest place, opened only a year ago, and my smallest, so it's not in an office building, it's an apartment—on account of the labor law. You can't have women working in an office building after two a.m. unless it's a public service, but I have to give my clients all-night service, so there on Sixty-ninth Street I've got four operators for the three switchboards, and they all live right there in the apartment. That way I can have one at the boards from eight till two at night, and another one from two o'clock on. After nine in the morning three are on, one for each board, for the daytime load."

"Are the switchboards installed in one of the rooms of the apartment?"

"Yes, sir."

"Tell the jury what one of them is like and how it works."

Bagby darted another nervous glance at the jury box and went back to the prosecutor. "It's a good deal like any board in a big office, with rows of holes for the plugs. Of course it's installed by the telephone company, with the special wiring for connections with my clients' phones. Each board has room for sixty clients. For each client there's a little light and a hole and a card strip with the client's name. When someone dials a client's number his light goes on and a buzz synchronizes with the ringing of the client's phone. How many buzzes the girl counts before she plugs in depends on what client it is. Some of them want her to plug in after three buzzes, some want her to wait longer. I've got one client that has her count fifteen buzzes. That's the kind of specialized individualized service I give my clients. The big outfits, the ones with tens of thousands of clients, they won't do that. They've commercialized it. With me every client is a special case and a sacred trust."

"Thank you, Mr. Bagby." Mandelbaum swiveled his head for a swift sympathetic smile at the jury and swiveled it back again. "But I wasn't buzzing for a plug for your business. When a client's light shows on the board, and the girl has heard the prescribed number of buzzes, she plugs in on the line, is that it?"

I thought Mandelbaum's crack was a little out of place for that setting, where a man was on trial for his life, and turned my head right for a glance at Nero Wolfe to see if he agreed, but one glimpse of his profile told me that he was sticking to his role of a morose martyr and so was in no humor to agree with anyone or anything.

That was to be expected. At that hour of the morning, following his hard-and-fast schedule, he would have been up in the plant rooms on the roof of his old brownstone house on West Thirty-fifth Street, bossing Theodore for the glory of his celebrated collection of orchids, even possibly getting his hands dirty. At eleven o'clock, after washing his hands, he would have taken the elevator down to his office on the ground floor, arranged his oversized corpus in his oversized chair behind his desk, rung for Fritz to bring beer, and started bossing Archie Goodwin, me. He would have given me any instructions he thought timely and desirable, for anything from typing a letter to tailing the mayor, which seemed likely to boost his income and add to his reputation as the best private detective east of San Francisco. And he would have been looking forward to lunch by Fritz.

And all that was "would-have-been" because he had been subpoenaed by the State of New York to appear in court and testify at the trial of Leonard Ashe. He hated to leave his house at all, and particularly he hated to leave it for a trip to a witness-box. Being a private detective, he had to concede that a summons to testify was an occupational hazard he must accept if he hoped to collect fees from clients, but this cloud didn't even have that silver lining. Leonard Ashe had come to the office one day about two months ago to hire him, but had been turned down. So neither fee nor glory was in prospect. As for me, I had been subpoenaed too, but only for insurance, since I wouldn't be called unless Mandelbaum decided Wolfe's testimony needed corroboration, which wasn't likely.

It was no pleasure to look at Wolfe's gloomy phiz, so I looked back at the performers. Bagby was answering. "Yes, sir, she plugs in and says, 'Mrs. Smith's residence,' or, 'Mr. Jones's apartment,' or whatever she has been told to say for that client. Then she says Mrs. Smith is out and is there any message, and so on, whatever the situation calls for. Sometimes the client has called and given her a message for some particular caller." Bagby flipped a hand. "Just anything. We give specialized service."

Mandelbaum nodded. "I think that gives us a clear picture of the operation. Now, Mr. Bagby, please look at that gentleman in the dark blue suit sitting next to the officer. He is the defendant in this trial. Do you know him?"

"Yes, sir. That's Mr. Leonard Ashe."

"When and where did you meet him?"

"In July he came to my office on Forty-seventh Street. First he phoned, and then he came."

"Can you give the day in July?"

"The twelfth. A Monday."

"What did he say?"

"He asked how my answering service worked, and I told him, and he said he wanted it for his home telephone at his apartment on East Seventy-third Street. He paid cash for a month in advance. He wanted twenty-four-hour service."

"Did he want any special service?"

"He didn't ask me for any, but two days later he contacted Marie Willis and offered her five hundred dollars if she—"

The witness was interrupted from two directions at once. The defense attorney, a champion named Jimmy Donovan whose batting average on big criminal cases had topped the list of the New York bar for ten years, left his chair with his mouth open to object; and Mandelbaum showed the witness a palm to stop him.

"Just a minute, Mr. Bagby. Just answer my questions. Did you accept Leonard Ashe as a client?"

"Sure, there was no reason not to."

"What was the number of his telephone at his home?"

"Rhinelander two-three-eight-three-eight."

"Did you give his name and that number a place on one of your switchboards?"

"Yes, sir, one of the three boards at the apartment on East Sixty-ninth Street. That's the Rhinelander district."

"What was the name of the employee who attended that board—the one with Leonard Ashe's number on it?"

"Marie Willis."

A shadow of stir and murmur rippled across the packed audience, and Judge Corbett on the bench turned his head to give it a frown and then went back to his knitting.

Bagby was going on. "Of course at night there's

only one girl on the three boards—they rotate on that —but for daytime I keep a girl at her own board at least five days a week, and six if I can. That way she gets to know her clients."

"And Leonard Ashe's number was on Marie Willis's board?"

"Yes, sir."

"After the routine arrangements for serving Leonard Ashe as a client had been completed, did anything happen to bring him or his number to your personal attention?"

"Yes, sir."

"What and when? First, when?"

Bagby took a second to make sure he had it right before swearing to it. "It was Thursday, three days after Ashe had ordered the service. That was July fifteenth. Marie phoned me at my office and said she wanted to see me privately about something important. I asked if it could wait till she was off the board at six o'clock, and she said yes, and a little after six I went up to Sixty-ninth Street and we went into her room at the apartment. She told me Ashe had phoned her the day before and asked her to meet him somewhere to discuss some details about servicing his number. She told him such a discussion should be with me, but he insisted—"

A pleasant but firm baritone cut in. "If Your Honor pleases." Jimmy Donovan was on his feet. "I submit that the witness may not testify to what Marie Willis and Mr. Ashe said to each other when he was not present."

"Certainly not," Mandelbaum agreed shortly. "He is reporting what Marie Willis told *him* had been said."

Judge Corbett nodded. "That should be kept clear. You understand that, Mr. Bagby?"

"Yes, sir." Bagby bit his lip. "I mean Your Honor."

"Then go ahead. What Miss Willis said to you and you to her."

"Well, she said she had agreed to meet Ashe because he was a theatrical producer and she wanted to be an actress. I hadn't known she was stage-struck but I know it now. So she had gone to his office on Forty-fifth Street as soon as she was off the board, and after he talked some and asked some questions he told her—this is what she told me—he told her he wanted her to listen in on calls to his home number during the daytime. All she would have to do, when his light on her board went on and the buzzes started, if the buzzes stopped and the light went off—that would mean someone had answered the phone at his home—she would plug in and listen to the conversation. Then each evening she would phone him and report. That's what she said Ashe had asked her to do. She said he counted out five hundred dollars in bills and offered them to her and told her he'd give her another thousand if she went along."

Bagby stopped for wind. Mandelbaum prodded him. "Did she say anything else?"

"Yes, sir. She said she knew she should have turned him down flat, but she didn't want to make him sore, so she told him she wanted to think it over for a day or two. Then she said she had slept on it and decided what to do. She said of course she knew that what Ashe was after was phone calls to his wife, and aside from anything else she wouldn't spy on his wife, because his wife was Robina Keane, who had given up her career as an actress two years ago to marry Ashe, and Marie worshiped Robina Keane as her ideal. That's what Marie told me. She said she had decided she must do three things. She must tell me about it because Ashe was my client and she was working for me. She must tell Robina Keane about it, to warn her, because Ashe would probably get someone else to do the spying for him. It occurred to me that her real reason for wanting to tell Robina Keane might be that she hoped—"

Mandelbaum stopped him. "What occurred to you isn't material, Mr. Bagby. Did Marie tell you the third thing she had decided she must do?"

"Yes, sir. That she must tell Ashe that she was going to tell his wife. She said she had to because at the start of her talk with him she had promised Ashe she would keep it confidential, so she had to warn him she was withdrawing her promise."

"Did she say when she intended to do those three things?"

The witness nodded. "She had already done one of them, telling me. She said she had phoned Ashe and told him she would be at his office at seven o'clock. That was crowding it a little, because she had the evening shift that day and would have to be back at the boards at eight o'clock. It crowded me too because it gave me no time to talk her out of it. I went downtown with her in a taxi, to Forty-fifth Street, where Ashe's office was, and did my best but couldn't move her."

"What did you say to her?"

"I tried to get her to lay off. If she went through with her program it might not do any harm to my business, but again it might. I tried to persuade her to let me handle it by going to Ashe and telling him she had told me of his offer and I didn't want him for a client, and then drop it and forget it, but she was dead set on warning Robina Keane, and to do that she had to withdraw her promise to Ashe. I hung on until she entered the elevator to go up to Ashe's office, but I couldn't budge her."

"Did you go up with her?"

"No, that wouldn't have helped any. She was going through with it, and what could I do?"

So, I was thinking to myself, that's how it is. It looked pretty tough to me, and I glanced at Wolfe, but his eyes were closed, so I turned my head the other way to see how the gentleman in the dark blue suit seated next to the officer was taking it. Apparently it looked pretty tough to Leonard Ashe too. With deep creases slanting along the jowls of his dark bony face from the corners of his wide full mouth, and his sunken dark eyes, he was certainly a prime subject for the artists who sketch candidates for the hot seat for the tabloids, and for three days they had been making the most of it. He was no treat for the eyes, and I took mine away from him, to the left, where his wife sat in the front row of the audience.

I had never worshiped Robina Keane as my ideal, but I had liked her fine in a couple of shows, and she was giving a good performance for her first and only courtroom appearance—either being steadfastly loyal to her husband or putting on an act, but good in either case. She was dressed quietly and she sat quietly, but she wasn't trying to pretend she wasn't young and beautiful. Exactly how she and her older and unbeautiful husband stood with each other was anybody's guess, and everybody was guessing. One extreme said he was her whole world and he had been absolutely batty to suspect her of any hoop-rolling; the other extreme said she had quit the stage only to have more time for certain promiscuous activities, and Ashe had been a sap not to know it sooner; and anywhere in between. I wasn't ready to vote. Looking at her, she might have been an angel. Looking at him, it must have taken something drastic to get him that miserable, though I granted that being locked up two months on a charge of murder would have some effect.

Mandelbaum was making sure the jury had got it. "Then you didn't go up to Ashe's office with Marie Willis?"

"No, sir."

"Did you go up later, at any time, after she had gone up?"

"No, sir."

"Did you see Ashe at all that evening?"

"No, sir."

"Did you speak to him on the telephone that evening?"

"No, sir."

Looking at Bagby, and I have looked at a lot of specimens under fire, I decided that either he was telling it straight or he was an expert liar, and he didn't sound like an expert. Mandelbaum went on. "What did you do that evening, after you saw Marie Willis enter the elevator to go up to Ashe's office?"

"I went to keep a dinner date with a friend at a restaurant—Hornby's on Fifty-second Street—and after that, around half-past eight, I went up to my Trafalgar office at Eighty-sixth Street and Broadway. I have six boards there, and a new night girl was on, and I stayed there with her a while and then took a taxi home, across the park to my apartment on East Seventieth Street. Not long after I got home a phone call came from the police to tell me Marie Willis had been found murdered in my Rhinelander office, and I went there as fast as I could go, and there was a crowd out in front, and an officer took me upstairs."

He stopped to swallow, and stuck his chin out a

little. "They hadn't moved her. They had taken the plug cord from around her throat, but they hadn't moved her, and there she was, slumped over on the ledge in front of the board. They wanted me to identify her, and I had—"

The witness wasn't interrupted, but I was. There was a tug at my sleeve, and a whisper in my ear— "We're leaving, come on." And Nero Wolfe arose, sidled past two pairs of knees to the aisle, and headed for the rear of the courtroom. For his bulk he could move quicker and smoother than you would expect, and as I followed him to the door and on out to the corridor we got no attention at all. I was assuming that some vital need had stirred him, like phoning Theodore to tell him or ask him something about an orchid, but he went on past the phone booths to the elevator and pushed the down button. With people all around I asked no questions. He got out at the main floor and made for Centre Street. Out on the sidewalk he backed up against the granite of the courthouse and spoke.

"We want a taxi, but first a word with you."

"No, sir," I said firmly. "First a word *from* me. Mandelbaum may finish with that witness any minute, and the cross-examination may not take long, or Donovan might even reserve it, and you were told you would follow Bagby. If you want a taxi, of course you're going home, and that will just—"

"I'm not going home. I can't."

"Right. If you do you'll merely get hauled back here and also a fat fine for contempt of court. Not to mention me. I'm under subpoena too. I'm going back to the courtroom. Where are you going?"

"To six-eighteen East Sixty-ninth Street."

I goggled at him. "I've always been afraid of this. Does it hurt?"

"Yes. I'll explain on the way."

"I'm going back to the courtroom."

"No. I'll need you."

Like everyone else, I love to feel needed, so I wheeled, crossed the sidewalk, flagged a taxi to the curb, and opened the door. Wolfe came and climbed in, and I followed. After he had got himself braced against the hazards of a carrier on wheels and I had given the driver the address, and we were rolling, I said, "Shoot. I've heard you do a lot of explaining, but this will have to be good."

"It's preposterous," he declared.

"It sure is. Let's go back."

"I mean Mr. Mandelbaum's thesis. I will concede that Mr. Ashe might have murdered that girl. I will concede that his state of mind about his wife might have approached mania, and therefore the motive suggested by that witness might have been adequate provocation. But he's not an imbecile. Under the circumstances as given, and I doubt if Mr. Bagby can be discredited, I refuse to believe he was ass enough to go to that place at that time and kill her. You were present when he called on me that day to hire me. Do you believe it?"

I shook my head. "I pass. You're explaining. However, I read the papers too, and also I've chatted with Lon Cohen of the *Gazette* about it. It doesn't have to be that Ashe went there for the purpose of killing her. His story is that a man phoned him—a voice he didn't recognize—and said if Ashe would meet him at the Bagby place on Sixty-ninth Street he thought they could talk Marie out of it, and Ashe went on the hop, and the door to the office was standing open, and he went in and there she was with a plug cord tight around her throat, and he opened a window and yelled for the police. Of course if you like it that Bagby was lying just now when he said it wasn't him that phoned Ashe, and that Bagby is such a good businessman that he would rather kill an employee than lose a customer—"

"Pfui. It isn't what I like, it's what I don't like. Another thing I didn't like was sitting there on that confounded wooden bench with a smelly woman against me. Soon I was going to be called as a witness, and my testimony would have been effective corroboration of Mr. Bagby's testimony, as you know. It was intolerable. I believe that if Mr. Ashe is convicted of murder on the thesis Mr. Mandelbaum is presenting it will be a justicial transgression, and I will not be a party to it. It wasn't easy to get up and go because I can't go home. If I go home they'll come and drag me out, and into that witness-box."

I eyed him. "Let's see if I get you. You can't bear to help convict Ashe of murder because you doubt if he's guilty, so you're scooting. Right?"

The hackie twisted his head around to inform us through the side of his mouth, "Sure he's guilty."

We ignored it. "That's close enough," Wolfe said.

"Not close enough for me. If you expect me to scoot with you and invite a stiff fine for running out on a subpoena, which you will pay, don't try to guff me. Say we doubt if Ashe is guilty, but we think he may get tagged because we know Mandelbaum wouldn't go to trial without a good case. Say also our bank account needs a shot in the arm, which is true. So we decide to see if we can find something that will push Mandelbaum's nose in, thinking that if Ashe is properly grateful a measly little fine will be nothing. The way to proceed would be for you to think up a batch of errands for me, and you go on home and read a book and have a good lunch, but that's out because they'd come and get you. Therefore we must both do errands. If that's how it stands, it's a fine day and I admit that woman was smelly, but I have a good nose and I think it was Tissot's Passion Flower, which is eighty bucks an ounce. What are we going to do at Sixty-ninth Street?"

"I don't know."

"Good. Neither do I."

II

It was a dump, an old five-story walk-up, brick that had been painted yellow about the time I had started working for Nero Wolfe. In the vestibule I pushed the button that was labeled *Bagby Answers, Inc.*, and when the click came I opened the door and led the way across the crummy little hall to the stairs and up one flight. Mr. Bagby wasn't wasting it on rent. At the front end of the hall a door stood open. As we approached it I stepped aside to let Wolfe go first, since I didn't know whether we were disguised as brush peddlers or as plumbers.

As Wolfe went to speak to a girl at a desk I sent my eyes on a quick survey. It was the scene of the murder. In the front wall of the room three windows overlooked the street. Against the opposite wall were ranged the three switchboards, with three females with headphones seated at them. They had turned their heads for a look at the company.

The girl at the desk, which was near the end window, had only an ordinary desk phone, in addition to a typewriter and other accessories. Wolfe was telling her, "My name is Wolfe and I've just come from the courtroom where Leonard Ashe is being tried." He indicated me with a jerk of his head. "This is my assistant, Mr. Goodwin. We're checking on subpoenas that have been served on witnesses, for both the prosecution and the defense. Have you been served?"

With his air and presence and tone, only one woman in a hundred would have called him, and she wasn't it. Her long, narrow face tilted up to him, she shook her head. "No, I haven't."

"Your name, please?"

"Pearl Fleming."

"Then you weren't working here on July fifteenth."

"No, I was at another office. There was no office desk here then. One of the boards took office calls."

"I see." His tone implied that it was damned lucky for her that he saw. "Are Miss Hart and Miss Velardi and Miss Weltz here?"

My brows wanted to lift, but I kept them down, and anyway there was nothing startling about it. True, it had been weeks since those names had appeared in the papers, but Wolfe never missed a word of an account of a murder, and his skull's filing system was even better than Saul Panzer's.

Pearl Fleming pointed to the switchboards. "That's Miss Hart at the end. Miss Velardi is next to her. Next to Miss Velardi is Miss Yerkes. She came after—she replaced Miss Willis. Miss Weltz isn't here; it's her day off. They've had subpoenas, but—"

She stopped and turned her head. The woman at the end board had removed her headphone, left her seat, and was marching over to us. She was about my age, with sharp brown eyes and flat cheeks and a chin she could have used for an icebreaker if she had been a walrus.

"Aren't you Nero Wolfe, the detective?" she demanded.

"Yes," he assented. "You are Alice Hart?"

She skipped it. "What do you want?"

Wolfe backed up a step. He doesn't like anyone so close to him, especially a woman. "I want information, madam. I want you and Bella Velardi and Helen Weltz to answer some questions."

"We have no information."

"Then I won't get any, but I'm going to try."

"Who sent you here?"

"Autokinesis. There's a cardinal flaw in the assumption that Leonard Ashe killed Marie Willis, and I don't like flaws. It has made me curious, and when I'm curious there is only one cure—the whole truth, and I intend to find it. If I am in time to save Mr. Ashe's life, so much the better; but in any case I have started and will not be stopped. If you and the others refuse to oblige me today there will be other days—and other ways."

From her face it was a toss-up. Her chin stiffened, and for a second she was going to tell him to go soak his head; then her eyes left him for me, and she was going to take it. She turned to the girl at the desk. "Take my board, will you, Pearl? I won't be long." To Wolfe, snapping it: "We'll go to my room. This way." She whirled and started.

"One moment, Miss Hart." Wolfe moved. "A point not covered in the newspaper accounts." He stopped at the boards, behind Bella Velardi at the middle one. "Marie Willis's body was found slumped over on the ledge in front of the switchboard. Presumably she was seated at the switchboard when the murderer arrived. But you live here—you and the others?"

"Yes."

"Then if the murderer was Mr. Ashe, how did he know she was alone on the premises?"

"I don't know: Perhaps she told him she was. Is that the flaw?"

"Good heavens, no. It's conceivable that she did, and they talked, and he waited until a light and buzzes had her busy at the board, with her back to him. It's a minor point, but I prefer someone with surer knowledge that she was alone. Since she was small and slight, even you are not excluded"—he wiggled a finger—"or these others. Not that I am now prepared to charge you with murder."

"I hope not," she snorted, turning. She led the way to a door at the end of the room, on through, and down a narrow hall. As I followed, behind Wolfe, I was thinking that the reaction we were getting seemed a little exaggerated. It would have been natural, under the circumstances, for Miss Velardi and Miss Yerkes to turn in their seats for a good look at us, but they hadn't. They had sat, rigid, staring at their boards. As for Alice Hart, either there had been a pinch of relief in her voice when she asked Wolfe if that was the flaw, or I was in the wrong business.

Her room was a surprise. First, it was big, much bigger than the one in front with the switchboards. Second, I am not Bernard Berenson, but I have noticed things here and there, and the framed splash of red and yellow and blue above the mantel was not only a real van Gogh, it was bigger and better than the one Lily Rowan had. I saw Wolfe spotting it as he lowered himself onto a chair actually big enough for him, and I pulled one around to make a group, facing the couch Miss Hart dropped onto.

As she sat she spoke. "What's the flaw?"

He shook his head. "I'm the inquisitor, Miss Hart,

not you." He aimed a thumb at the van Gogh. "Where did you get that picture?"

She looked at it, and back at him. "That's none of your business."

"It certainly isn't. But here is the situation. You have of course been questioned by the police and the District Attorney's office, but they were restrained by their assumption that Leonard Ashe was the culprit. Since I reject that assumption and must find another in its stead, there can be no limit to my impertinence with you and others who may be involved. Take you and that picture. If you refuse to say where you got it, or if your answer doesn't satisfy me, I'll put a man on it, a competent man, and he'll find out. You can't escape being badgered, madam; the question is whether you suffer it here and now, by me, or face a prolonged inquiry among your friends and associates by meddlesome men. If you prefer the latter don't waste time with me; I'll go and tackle one of the others."

She was tossing up again. From her look at him it seemed just as well that he had his bodyguard along. She tried stalling. "What does it matter where I got that picture?"

"Probably it doesn't. Possibly nothing about you matters. But the picture is a treasure, and this is an odd address for it. Do you own it?"

"Yes. I bought it."

"When?"

"About a year ago. From a dealer."

"The contents of this room are yours?"

"Yes. I like things that—well, this is my extravagance, my only one."

"How long have you been with this firm?"

"Five years."

"What is your salary?"

She was on a tight rein. "Eighty dollars a week."

"Not enough for your extravagance. An inheritance? Alimony? Other income?"

"I have never married. I had some savings, and I wanted—I wanted these things. If you save for fifteen years you have a right to something."

"You have indeed. Where were you the evening that Marie Willis was killed?"

"I was out in Jersey, in a car with a friend—Bella Velardi. To get cooled off—it was a hot night. We got back after midnight."

"In your car?"

"No, Helen Weltz had let us take hers. She has a Jaguar."

My brows went up, and I spoke. "A Jaguar," I told Wolfe, "is quite a machine. You couldn't squeeze into one. Counting taxes and extras, four thousand bucks isn't enough."

His eyes darted to me and back to her. "Of course the police have asked if you know of anyone who might have had a motive for killing Marie Willis. Do you?"

"No." Her rein wasn't so tight.

"Were you friendly with her?"

"Yes, friendly enough."

"Has any client ever asked you to listen in on calls to his number?"

"Certainly not!"

"Did you know Miss Willis wanted to be an actress?"

"Yes, we all knew that."

"Mr. Bagby says he didn't."

Her chin had relaxed a little. "He was her employer. I don't suppose he knew. When did you talk with Mr. Bagby?"

"I didn't. I heard him on the witness stand. Did you know of Miss Willis's regard for Robina Keane?"

"Yes, we all knew that too. Marie did imitations of Robina Keane in her parts."

"When did she tell you of her decision to tell Robina Keane that her husband was going to monitor her telephone?"

Miss Hart frowned. "I didn't say she told me."

"Did she?"

"No."

"Did anyone?"

"Yes, Miss Velardi. Marie had told her. You can ask her."

"I shall. Do you know Guy Unger?"

"Yes, I know him. Not very well."

Wolfe was playing a game I had often watched him at, tossing balls at random to see how they bounced. It's a good way to try to find a lead if you haven't got one, but it may take all day, and he didn't have it. If one of the females in the front room took a notion to phone the cops or the DA's office about us we might have visitors any minute. As for Guy Unger, that was another name from the newspaper accounts. He had been Marie Willis's boy friend, or had he? There had been a difference of opinion among the journalists.

Miss Hart's opinion was that Guy Unger and Marie had enjoyed each other's company, but that was as far as it went—I mean her opinion. She knew nothing of any crisis that might have made Unger want to end the friendship with a plug cord. For another five minutes Wolfe went on with the game, tossing different balls from different angles, and then abruptly arose.

"Very well," he said. "For now. I'll try Miss Velardi."

"I'll send her in." Alice Hart was on her feet, eager

to cooperate. "Her room is next door." She moved. "This way."

Obviously she didn't want to leave us with her van Gogh. There was a lock on a bureau drawer that I could probably have manipulated in twenty seconds, and I would have liked to try my hand on it, but Wolfe was following her out, so I went along—to the right, down the hall to another door, standing open. Leaving us there, she strode on flat heels toward the front. Wolfe passed through the open door with me behind.

This room was different—somewhat smaller, with no van Gogh and the kind of furniture you might expect. The bed hadn't been made, and Wolfe stood and scowled at it a moment, lowered himself gingerly onto a chair too small for him with worn upholstery, and told me curtly, "Look around."

I did so. Bella Velardi was a crack-lover. A closet door and a majority of the drawers in a dressing table and two chests were open to cracks of various widths. One of the reasons I am still shy a wife is the risk of getting a crack-lover. I went and pulled the closet door open, and, having no machete to hack my way into the jungle of duds, swung it back to its crack and stepped across to the library. It was a stack of paperbacks on a little table, the one on top being entitled *One Mistake Too Many*, with a picture of a double-breasted floozie shrinking in terror from a muscle-bound baboon. There was also a pile of recent editions of *Racing Form* and *Track Dope*.

"She's a philanthropist," I told Wolfe. "She donates dough to the cause of equine genetics."

"Meaning?"

"She bets on horse races."

"Does she lose much?"

"She loses. How much depends on what she bets.

Probably tidy sums, since she takes two house journals."

He grunted. "Open drawers. Have one open when she enters. I want to see how much impudence these creatures will tolerate."

I obeyed. The six drawers in the bigger chest all held clothes, and I did no pawing. A good job might have uncovered some giveaway under a pile of nylons, but there wasn't time for it. I closed all the drawers to show her what I thought of cracks. Those in the dressing table were also uninteresting. In the second drawer of the smaller chest, among other items, was a collection of photographs, mostly unmounted snaps, and, running through them, with no expectations, I stopped at one for a second look. It was Bella Velardi and another girl, with a man standing between them, in bathing outfits with the ocean for background. I went and handed it to Wolfe.

"The man?" I asked. "I read newspapers too, and look at the pictures, but it was two months ago, and I could be wrong."

He slanted it to get the best light from a window. He nodded. "Guy Unger." He slipped it into a pocket. "Find more of him."

"If any." I went back to the collection. "But you may not get a chance at her. It's been a good four minutes. Either she's getting a full briefing from Miss Hart, or they've phoned for help, and in that case—"

The sound came of high heels clicking on the uncarpeted hall. I closed the second drawer and pulled the third one open, and was inspecting its contents when the clicks got to the door and were in the room. Shutting it in no hurry and turning to Bella Velardi, I was ready to meet a yelp of indignation, but didn't have to. With her snappy black eyes and sassy little face she must have been perfectly capable of indignation, but her nerves were too busy with something else. She decided to pretend she hadn't caught me with a drawer open, and that was screwy. Added to other things, it made it a cinch that these phone answerers had something on their minds.

Bella Velardi said in a scratchy little voice, "Miss Hart says you want to ask me something," and went and sat on the edge of the unmade bed, with her fingers twisted together.

Wolfe regarded her with his eyes half closed. "Do you know what a hypothetical question is, Miss Velardi?"

"Of course I do."

"I have one for you. If I put three expert investigators on the job of finding out approximately how much you have lost betting on horse races in the past year, how long do you think it would take them?"

"Why, I—" She blinked at him with a fine set of long lashes. "I don't know."

"I do. With luck, five hours. Without it, five days. It would be simpler for you to tell me. How much have you lost?"

She blinked again. "How do you know I've lost anything?"

"I don't. But Mr. Goodwin, who is himself an expert investigator, concluded from publications he found on that table that you are a chronic bettor. If so, there's a fair chance that you keep a record of your gains and losses." He turned to me. "Archie, your search was interrupted. Resume. See if you can find it." Back to her. "At his elbow if you like, Miss Velardi. There is no question of pilfering."

I went to the smaller chest. He was certainly crowding his luck. If she took this without calling a cop she might not be a murderess, but she sure had a tender spot she didn't want touched.

Actually she didn't just sit and take it. As I got a drawer handle to pull it open she loosened her tongue. "Look, Mr. Wolfe, I'm perfectly willing to tell you anything you want to know. Perfectly!" She was leaning toward him, her fingers still twisted. "Miss Hart said I mustn't be surprised at anything you asked, but I was, so I guess I was flustered. There's no secret about my liking to bet on the races, but the amounts I bet— that's different. You see, I have friends who—well, they don't want people to know they bet, so they give me money to bet for them. So it's about a hundred dollars a week, sometimes more, maybe up to two hundred."

If she liked to bet on any animals other than horses, one would have got her ten that she was a damn liar. Evidently Wolfe would have split it with me, since he didn't even bother to ask her the names of the friends.

He merely nodded. "What is your salary?"

"It's only sixty-five, so of course I can't bet much myself."

"Of course. About the windows in that front room. In summer weather, when one of you is on duty there at night, are the windows open?"

She was concentrating. "When it's hot, yes. Usually the one in the middle. If it's very hot, maybe all of them."

"With the shades up?"

"Yes."

"It was hot July fifteenth. Were the windows open that night?"

"I don't know. I wasn't here."

"Where were you?"

"I was out in Jersey, in a car with a friend—Alice Hart. To get cooled off. We got back after midnight."

Wonderful, I thought. That settled that. One woman might conceivably lie, but surely not two.

Wolfe was eying her. "If the windows were open and the shades up the evening of July fifteenth, as they almost certainly were, would anyone in her senses have proceeded to kill Marie Willis so exposed to view? What do you think?"

She didn't call him on the pronoun. "Why, no," she conceded. "That would have been—no, I don't think so."

"Then she—or he—must have closed the windows and drawn the shades before proceeding. How could Leonard Ashe, in the circumstances as given, have managed that without alarming Miss Willis?"

"I don't know. He might have—no, I don't know."

"He might have what?"

"Nothing. I don't know."

"How well do you know Guy Unger?"

"I know him fairly well."

She had been briefed all right. She was expecting that one.

"Have you seen much of him in the past two months?"

"No, very little."

Wolfe reached in his pocket and got the snapshot and held it out. "When was this taken?"

She left the bed and was going to take it, but he held on to it. After a look she said, "Oh, that," and sat down again. All of a sudden she exploded, indignation finally breaking through. "You took that from my drawer! What else did you take?" She sprang up, trembling all over. "Get out of here! Get out and stay out!"

Wolfe returned the snap to his pocket, arose, said,

"Come, Archie, there seems to be a limit after all," and
started for the door. I followed.

He was at the sill when she darted past me,
grabbed his arm, and took it back. "Wait a minute, I
didn't mean that. I flare up like that. I just—I don't
care about the damn picture."

Wolfe pulled loose and got a yard of space. "When
was it taken?"

"About two weeks ago—two weeks ago Sunday."

"Who is the other woman?"

"Helen Weltz."

"Who took it?"

"A man that was with us."

"His name?"

"His name is Ralph Ingalls."

"Was Guy Unger Miss Weltz's companion, or
yours?"

"Why, we—we were just together."

"Nonsense. Two men and two women are never
just together. How were you paired?"

"Well—Guy and Helen, and Ralph and me."

Wolfe sent a glance at the chair he had vacated and
apparently decided it wasn't worth the trouble of walking back to it. "Then since Miss Willis died Mr. Unger's
interest has centered on Miss Weltz?"

"I don't know about 'centered.' They seem to like
each other, as far as I know."

"How long have you been working here?"

"At this office, since it opened a year ago. Before
that I was at the Trafalgar office for two years."

"When did Miss Willis tell you she was going to tell
Robina Keane of her husband's proposal?"

She had expected that one too. "That morning.
That Thursday, the fifteenth of July."

"Did you approve?"

"No, I didn't. I thought she ought to just tell him no and forget it. I told her she was asking for trouble and she might get it. But she was so daddled on Robina Keane—" Bella shrugged. "Do you want to sit down?"

"No, thank you. Where is Miss Weltz?"

"This is her day off."

"I know. Where can I find her?"

She opened her mouth and closed it. She opened it again. "I'm not sure. Wait a minute," she said, and went clicking down the hall to the front. It was more like two minutes when she came clicking back and reported, "Miss Hart thinks she's at a little place she rented for the summer up in Westchester. Do you want me to phone and find out?"

"Yes, if you would."

Off she went, and we followed. In the front room the other three were at the boards. While Bella Velardi spoke to Miss Hart, and Miss Hart went to the phone at the desk and got a number and talked, Wolfe stood and frowned around, at the windows, the boards, the phone answerers, and me. When Miss Hart told him Helen Weltz was on the wire he went to the desk and took it.

"Miss Weltz? This is Nero Wolfe. As Miss Hart told you, I'm looking into certain matters connected with the murder of Marie Willis, and would like to see you. I have some other appointments but can adjust them. How long will it take you to get to the city? . . . You can't? . . . I'm afraid I can't wait until tomorrow. . . . No, that's out of the question. . . . I see. You'll be there all afternoon? . . . Very well, I'll do that."

He hung up and asked Miss Hart to tell me how to get to the place in Westchester. She obliged, and beyond Katonah it got so complicated that I got out my notebook. Also I jotted down the phone number. Wolfe had marched out with no amenities, so I thanked her politely and caught up with him halfway down the stairs. When we were out on the sidewalk I inquired, "A taxi to Katonah?"

"No." He was cold with rage. "To the garage for the car."

We headed west.

III

As we stood inside the garage, on Thirty-sixth Street near Tenth Avenue, waiting for Pete to bring the car down, Wolfe came out with something I had been expecting.

"We could walk home," he said, "in four minutes."

I gave him a grin. "Yes, sir. I knew it was coming— while you were on the phone. To go to Katonah we would have to drive. To drive we would have to get the car. To get the car we would have to come to the garage. The garage is so close to home that we might as well go and have lunch first. Once in the house, with the door bolted and not answering the phone, we could reconsider the matter of driving to Westchester. So you told her we would go to Katonah."

"No. It occurred to me in the cab."

"I can't prove it didn't. But I have a suggestion." I nodded at the door to the garage office. "There's a phone in there. Call Fritz first. Or shall I?"

"I suppose so," he muttered, and went to the office door and entered, sat at the desk, and dialed. In a moment he was telling Fritz who and where he was, asking some questions, and getting answers he didn't like. After instructing Fritz to tell callers that he hadn't heard from us and had no idea where we were, and telling him not to expect us home until we got there, he hung up, glared at the phone, and then glared at me.

"There have been four phone calls. One from an officer of the court, one from the District Attorney's office, and two from Inspector Cramer."

"Ouch." I made a face. "The court and the DA, sure, but not Cramer. When you're within a mile of a homicide of his he itches from head to foot. You can imagine what kind of suspicions your walking out under a subpoena would give him. Let's go home. It will be interesting to see whether he has one dick posted out in front, or two or three. Of course he'll collar you and you may get no lunch at all, but what the hell."

"Shut up."

"Yes, sir. Here comes the car."

As we emerged from the office the brown sedan rolled to a stop before us and Pete got out and opened the rear door for Wolfe, who refuses to ride in front because when the crash comes the broken glass will carve him up. I climbed in behind the wheel, released the brake and fingered the lever, and fed gas.

At that time of day the West Side Highway wasn't too crowded, and north of Henry Hudson Bridge, and then on the Sawmill River Parkway, there was nothing to it. I could have let my mind roam if it had had anywhere to roam, but where? I was all for earning a little token of gratitude by jerking Leonard Ashe out from under, but how? It was so damn childish. In his own comfortable chair in his office, Wolfe could usually manage to keep his genius under control, but on the hard courtroom bench, with a perfumed woman crowded against him, knowing he couldn't get up and go home, he had dropped the reins, and now he was stuck. He couldn't call it off and go back to court and apologize because he was too darned pigheaded. He couldn't go home. There was even a chance he couldn't go to Katonah for a wild goose. When I saw in the rear-view mirror a parkway police car closing in on us from behind, I tightened my lips, and when he passed on by and shot ahead I relaxed and took a deep breath. It would have been pretty extreme to broadcast a general alarm for a mere witness AWOL, but the way Cramer felt about Wolfe it wouldn't have been fantastic.

As I slowed down for Hawthorne Circle I told Wolfe it was a quarter to two and I was hungry and what about him, and was instructed to stop somewhere and get cheese and crackers and beer, and a little farther on I obeyed. Parked off a side road, he ate the crackers and drank the beer, but rejected the cheese after one taste. I was too hungry to taste.

The dash clock said 2:38 when, having followed Alice Hart's directions, I turned off a dirt road into a narrow rutted driveway, crawled between thick bushes on both sides, and, reaching an open space, stepped on the brake to keep from rubbing a bright yellow Jaguar. To the left was a gravel walk across some grass that needed mowing, leading to a door in the side of a little white house with blue trim. As I climbed out two people appeared around the corner of the house. The one in front was the right age, the right size, and the right shape, with blue eyes and hair that matched the Jaguar, held back smooth with a yellow ribbon.

She came on. "You're Archie Goodwin? I'm Helen Weltz. Mr. Wolfe? It's a pleasure. This is Guy Unger. Come this way. We'll sit in the shade of the old apple tree."

In my dim memory of his picture in the paper two months back, and in the snap I had found in Bella Velardi's drawer, Guy Unger hadn't looked particularly like a murderer, and in the flesh he didn't fill the bill any better. He looked too mean, with mean little eyes in a big round face. His gray suit had been cut by someone who knew how, to fit his bulgy shoulders, one a little lower than the other. His mouth, if he had opened it wide, would have been just about big enough to poke his thumb in.

The apple tree was from colonial times, with windfalls of its produce scattered around. Wolfe glowered at the chairs with wooden slats which had been painted white the year before, but it was either that or squat, so he engineered himself into one. Helen Weltz asked what we would like to drink, naming four choices, and Wolfe said no, thank you, with cold courtesy. It didn't seem to faze her. She took a chair facing him, gave him a bright, friendly smile, and included me with a glance from her lively blue eyes.

"You didn't give me a chance on the phone," she said, not complaining. "I didn't want you to have a trip for nothing. I can't tell you anything about that awful business, what happened to Marie. I really can't, because I don't know anything. I was out on the Sound on a boat. Didn't she tell you?"

Wolfe grunted. "That's not the kind of thing I'm after, Miss Weltz. Such routine matters as checking alibis have certainly been handled competently by the police, to the limit of their interest. My own interest has been engaged late—I hope not too late—and my attack must be eccentric. For instance, when did Mr. Unger get here?"

"Why, he just—"

"Now, wait a minute." Unger had picked up an unfinished highball from a table next to him and was holding it with the fingertips of both hands. His voice wasn't squeaky, as you would expect, but a thick baritone. "Just forget me. I'm looking on, that's all. I can't say I'm an impartial observer, because I'm partial to Miss Weltz, if that's all right with her."

Wolfe didn't even glance at him. "I'll explain, Miss Weltz, why I ask when Mr. Unger got here. I'll explain fully. When I went to that place on Sixty-ninth Street and spoke with Miss Hart and Miss Velardi I was insufferable, both in manner and in matter, and they should have flouted me and ordered me out, but they didn't. Manifestly they were afraid to, and I intend to learn why. I assume that you know why. I assume that, after I left, Miss Hart phoned you again, described the situation, and discussed with you how best to handle me. I surmise that she also phoned Mr. Unger, or you did, and he was enough concerned about me to hurry to get here before I arrived. Naturally I would consider that significant. It would reinforce my suspicion that—"

"Forget it," Unger cut in. "I heard about you being on your way about ten minutes ago, when I got here. Miss Weltz invited me yesterday to come out this afternoon. I took a train to Katonah, and a taxi."

Wolfe looked at him. "I can't challenge that, Mr. Unger, but it doesn't smother my surmise. On the contrary. I'll probably finish sooner with Miss Weltz if you'll withdraw. For twenty minutes, say?"

"I think I'd better stay."

"Then please don't prolong it with interruptions."

"You behave yourself, Guy," Helen scolded him. She smiled at Wolfe. "I'll tell you what I think, I think he just wants to show you how smart he is. When I told him Nero Wolfe was coming you should have heard him! He said maybe you're famous for brains and he isn't, but he'd like to hear you prove it, something like that. I don't pretend to have brains. I was just scared!"

"Scared of what, Miss Weltz?"

"Scared of you! Wouldn't anybody be scared if they knew you were coming to pump them?" She was appealing to him.

"Not enough to send for help." Wolfe wouldn't enter into the spirit of it. "Certainly not if they had the alternative of snubbing me, as you have. Why don't you choose it? Why do you suffer me?"

"Now *that's* a question." She laughed. "I'll show you why." She got up and took a step, and reached to pat him on the shoulder and then on top of the head. "I didn't want to miss a chance to touch the great Nero Wolfe!" She laughed again, moved to the table and poured herself a healthy dose of bourbon, returned to her chair, and swallowed a good half of it. She shook herself and said, "Brrrrr. That's why!"

Unger was frowning at her. It didn't need the brains of a Nero Wolfe, or even a Guy Unger, to see that her nerves were teetering on an edge as sharp as a knife blade.

"But," Wolfe said dryly, "having touched me, you still suffer me. Of course Miss Hart told you that I reject the thesis that Leonard Ashe killed Marie Willis and propose to discredit it. I'm too late to try any of the conventional lines of inquiry, and anyway they have all been fully and competently explored by the police and the District Attorney on one side and Mr. Ashe's lawyer on the other. Since I can't expect to prove Mr. Ashe's innocence, the best I can hope to establish is a reasonable doubt of his guilt. Can you give it to me?"

"Of course not. How could I?"

"One way would be to suggest someone else with

motive and opportunity. Means is no problem, since the plug cord was there at hand. Can you?"

She giggled, and then was shocked, presumably at herself for giggling about murder. "Sorry," she apologized, "but you're funny. The way they had us down there at the District Attorney's office, and the way they kept after us, asking all about Marie and everybody she knew, and of course what they wanted was to find out if there was anybody besides that man Ashe that might have killed her. But now they're trying Ashe for it, and they wouldn't be trying him if they didn't think they could prove it, and here you come and expect to drag it out of me in twenty minutes. Don't you think that's funny for a famous detective like you? I do."

She picked up her glass and drained it, stiffened to control a shudder, and got up and started for the table. Guy Unger reached and beat her to the bottle. "You've had enough, Helen," he told her gruffly. "Take it easy." She stared down at him a moment, dropped the glass on his lap, and went back to her chair.

Wolfe eyed her. "No, Miss Weltz," he said. "No, I didn't expect to drag a disclosure from you in twenty minutes. The most I expected was support for my belief that you people have common knowledge of something that you don't want revealed, and you have given me that. Now I'll go to work, and I confess I'm not too sanguine. It's quite possible that after I've squandered my resources on it, time and thought and money and energy, and enlisted the help of half a dozen able investigators, I'll find that the matter you people are so nervous about has no bearing on the murder of Marie Willis and so is of no use to me, and of no concern. But I can't know that until I know what it is, so I'm going to know. If you think my process of finding out will cause inconvenience to you and the others, or worse, I suggest that you tell me now. It will—"

"I have nothing to tell you!"

"Nonsense. You're at the edge of hysteria."

"I am not!"

"Take it easy, Helen." Guy Unger focused his mean little eyes on Wolfe. "Look, I don't get this. As I understand it, what you're after is an out for Leonard Ashe on the murder. Is that right?"

"Yes."

"And that's all?"

"Yes."

"Would you mind telling me, did Ashe's lawyer hire you?"

"No."

"Who did?"

"Nobody. I developed a distaste for my function as a witness for the prosecution, along with a doubt of Mr. Ashe's guilt."

"Why doubt his guilt?"

Wolfe's shoulders went up a fraction of an inch, and down again. "Divination. Contrariety."

"I see." Unger pursed his midget mouth, which didn't need pursing. "You're shooting at it on spec." He leaned forward. "Understand me, I don't say that's not your privilege. Of course you have no standing at all, since you admit nobody hired you, but if Miss Weltz tells you to go to hell that won't take you off her neck if you've decided to go to town. She'll answer anything you want to ask her that's connected with the murder, and so will I. We've told the police and the District Attorney, why not you? Do you regard me as a suspect?"

"Yes."

"Okay." He leaned back. "I first met Marie Willis

about a year ago, a little more. I took her out a few times, maybe once a month, and then later a little oftener, to dinner and a show. We weren't engaged to be married, nothing like that. The last week in June, just two weeks before her death, she was on vacation, and four of us went for a cruise on my boat, up the Hudson and Lake Champlain. The other two were friends of mine, a man and a woman—do you want their names?"

"No."

"Well, that was what got me in the murder picture, that week's cruise she had taken on my boat so recently. There was nothing to it, we had just gone to have a good time, but when she was murdered the cops naturally thought I was a good prospect. There was absolutely nothing in my relations with Marie that could possibly have made me want to kill her. Any questions?"

"No."

"And if they had dug up a motive they would have been stuck with it, because I certainly didn't kill her the evening of July fifteenth. That was a Thursday, and at five o'clock that afternoon I was taking my boat through the Harlem River and into the sound, and at ten o'clock that night I was asleep on her at an anchorage near New Haven. My friend Ralph Ingalls was with me, and his wife, and Miss Helen Weltz. Of course the police have checked it, but maybe you don't like the way they check alibis. You're welcome to check it yourself if you care to. Any questions?"

"One or two." Wolfe shifted his fanny on the board slats. "What is your occupation?"

"For God's sake. You haven't even read the papers."

"Yes, I have, but that was weeks ago, and as I remember it they were vague. 'Broker,' I believe. Stock-broker?"

"No, I'm a freewheeler. I'll handle almost anything."

"Have you an office?"

"I don't need one."

"Have you handled any transactions for anyone connected with that business, Bagby Answers, Incorporated? Any kind of transaction?"

Unger cocked his head. "Now that's a funny question. Why do you ask that?"

"Because I suspect the answer is yes."

"Why? Just for curiosity."

"Now, Mr. Unger." Wolfe turned a palm up. "Since apparently you had heard of me, you may know that I dislike riding in cars, even when Mr. Goodwin is driving. Do you suppose I would have made this excursion completely at random? If you find the question embarrassing, don't answer it."

"It's not embarrassing." Unger turned to the table, poured an inch of bourbon in his glass, added two inches of water from a pitcher, gave it a couple of swirls, took a sip, and another one, and finally put the glass down and turned back to Wolfe.

"I'll tell you," he said in a new tone. "This whole business is pretty damn silly. I think you've got hold of some crazy idea somewhere, God knows what, and I want to speak with you privately." He arose. "Let's take a little walk."

Wolfe shook his head. "I don't like conversing on my feet. If you want to say something without a witness, Miss Weltz and Mr. Goodwin can leave us. Archie?"

I stood up. Helen Weltz looked up at Unger, and at me, and then slowly lifted herself from her chair.

"Let's go and pick flowers," I suggested. "Mr. Unger will want me in sight and out of hearing."

She moved. We picked our way through the windfalls of the apple tree, and of two more trees, and went on into a meadow where the grass and other stuff was up to our knees. She was in the lead. "Goldenrod I know," I told her back, "but what are the blue ones?"

No answer. In another hundred yards I tried again. "This is far enough unless he uses a megaphone."

She kept going. "Last call!" I told her. "I admit he would be a maniac to jump Mr. Wolfe under the circumstances, but maybe he is one. I learned long ago that with people involved in a murder case nothing is impossible."

She wheeled on me. "He's not involved in a murder case!"

"He will be before Mr. Wolfe gets through with him."

She plumped down in the grass, crossed her legs, buried her face in her hands, and started to shake. I stood and looked down at her, expecting the appropriate sound effect, but it didn't come. She just went on shaking, which wasn't wholesome. After half a minute of it I squatted in front of her, made contact by taking a firm grip on her bare ankle, and spoke with authority.

"That's no way to do it. Open a valve and let it out. Stretch out and kick and scream. If Unger thinks it's me and flies to the rescue that will give me an excuse to plug him."

She mumbled something. Her hands muffled it, but it sounded like "God help me." The shakes turned into shivers and were tapering off. When she spoke again it came through much better. "You're hurting me," she said, and I loosened my grip on her ankle and in a moment took my hand away, when her hands dropped and she lifted her head.

Her face was flushed, but her eyes were dry. "My God," she said, "it would be wonderful if you put your arms around me tight and told me, 'All right, my darling, I'll take care of everything, just leave it to me.' Oh, that would be wonderful!"

"I may try it," I offered, "if you'll brief me on what I'd have to take care of. The arms around you tight are no problem. Then what?"

She skipped over it. "God," she said bitterly, "am I a fool! You saw my car. My Jaguar."

"Yeah, I saw it. Very fine."

"I'm going to burn it. How do you set fire to a car?"

"Pour gasoline on it, all over inside, toss a match in, and jump back fast. Be careful what you tell the insurance company or you'll end up in the can."

She skipped again. "It wasn't only the car, it was other things too. I had to have them. Why didn't I get me a man? I could have had a dozen, but no, not me. I was going to do it all myself. It was going to be *my* Jaguar. And now here I am, and you, a man I never saw before—it would be heaven if you'd just take me over. I'm telling you, you'd be getting a bargain!"

"I might, at that." I was sympathetic but not mealy. "Don't be too sure you're a bad buy. What are the liabilities?"

She twisted her neck to look across the meadow toward the house. Wolfe and Unger were in their chairs under the apple tree, evidently keeping their voices down, since no sound came, and my ears are good.

She turned back to me. "Is it a bluff? Is he just trying to scare something out of us?"

"No, not just. If he scares something out, fine. If

not, he'll get it the hard way. If there's anything to get he'll get it. If you're sitting on a lid you don't want opened, my advice is to move, the sooner the better, or you may get hurt."

"I'm already hurt!"

"Then hurt worse."

"I guess I can be." She reached for one of the blue flowers and pulled it off with no stem. "You asked what these are. They're wild asters, just the color of my eyes." She crushed it with her fingers and dropped it. "I already know what I'm going to do. I decided walking over here with you. What time is it?"

I looked at my wrist. "Quarter past three."

"Let's see, four hours—five. Where can I see Nero Wolfe around nine o'clock in town?"

From long habit I started to say at his office, but remembered it was out of bounds. "His address and number are in the phone book," I told her, "but he may not be there this evening. Phone and ask for Fritz. Tell him you are the Queen of Hearts, and he'll tell you where Mr. Wolfe is. If you don't say you're the Queen of Hearts he won't tell you anything because Mr. Wolfe hates to be disturbed when he's out. But why not save time and trouble? Evidently you've decided to tell him something, and there he is. Come on and tell him now."

She shook her head. "I can't. I don't dare."

"On account of Unger?"

"Yes."

"If he can ask to speak privately with Mr. Wolfe, why can't you?"

"I tell you I don't dare!"

"We'll go and come back as soon as Unger leaves."

"He's not going to leave. He's going to ride to town with me."

"Then record it on tape and use me for tape. You

can trust my memory. I guarantee to repeat it to Mr.
Wolfe word for word. Then when you phone this evening he will have had time—"

"Helen! *Helen!*" Unger was calling her.

She started to scramble up, and I got upright and
gave her a hand. As we headed across the meadow she
spoke, barely above a whisper. "If you tell him I'll
deny it. Are you going to tell him?"

"Wolfe, yes. Unger, no."

"If you do I'll deny it."

"Then I won't."

As we approached they left their chairs. Their expressions indicated that they had not signed a mutual
nonaggression pact, but there were no scars of battle.
Wolfe said, "We're through here, Archie," and was going. Nobody else said anything, which made it rather
stiff. Following Wolfe around the house to the open
space, I saw that it would take a lot of maneuvering to
turn around without scraping the Jaguar, so I had to
back out through the bushes to the dirt road, where I
swung the rear around to head the way we had come.

When we had gone half a mile I called back to my
rearseat passenger, "I have a little item for you!"

"Stop somewhere," he ordered, louder than necessary. "I can't talk like this."

A little farther on there was roadside room under a
tree, and I pulled over and parked.

I twisted around in the seat to face him. "We got a
nibble," I said, and reported on Helen Weltz. He
started frowning, and when I finished he was frowning
more.

"Confound it," he growled, "she was in a panic, and
it'll wear off."

"It may," I conceded. "And so? I'll go back and do it
over if you'll write me a script."

"Pfui. I don't say I could better it. You are a connoisseur of comely young women. Is she a murderess in a funk trying to wriggle out? Or what is she?"

I shook my head. "I pass. She's trying to wriggle all right, but for out of what I would need six guesses. What did Unger want privately? Is he trying to wriggle too?"

"Yes. He offered me money—five thousand dollars, and then ten thousand."

"For what?"

"Not clearly defined. A retaining fee for investigative services. He was crude about it for a man with brains."

"I'll be damned." I grinned at him. "I've often thought you ought to get around more. Only five hours ago you marched out of that courtroom in the interest of justice, and already you've scared up an offer of ten grand. Of course it may have nothing to do with the murder. What did you tell him?"

"That I resented and scorned his attempt to suborn me."

My brows went up. "He was in a panic, and it'll wear off. Why not string him along?"

"It would take time, and I haven't any. I told him I intend to appear in court tomorrow morning."

"Tomorrow?" I stared. "With what, for God's sake?"

"At the least, with a diversion. If Miss Weltz's panic endures, possibly with something better, though I didn't know that when I was talking with Mr. Unger."

I looked it over. "Uh-huh," I said finally. "You've had a hard day, and soon it will be dark and dinnertime, and then bedtime, and deciding to go back to court tomorrow makes it possible for you to go home. Okay, I'll get you there by five o'clock."

I turned and reached for the ignition key, but had barely touched it when his voice stopped me. "We're not going home. Mr. Cramer will have a man posted there all night, probably with a warrant, and I'm not going to risk it. I had thought of a hotel, but that might be risky too, and now that Miss Weltz may want to see me it's out of the question. Isn't Saul's apartment conveniently located?"

"Yes, but he has only one bed. Lily Rowan has plenty of room in her penthouse, and we'd be welcome, especially you. You remember the time she squirted perfume on you."

"I do," he said coldly. "We'll manage somehow at Saul's. Besides, we have errands to do and may need him. We must of course phone him first. Go ahead. To the city."

He gripped the strap. I started the engine.

IV

For more years than I have fingers Inspector Cramer of Homicide had been dreaming of locking Wolfe up, at least overnight, and that day he darned near made it. He probably would have if I hadn't spent an extra dime. Having phoned Saul Panzer, and also Fritz, from a booth in a drugstore in Washington Heights, I called the *Gazette* office and got Lon Cohen. When he heard my voice he said, "Well, well. Are you calling from your cell?"

"No. If I told you where I am you'd be an accomplice. Has our absence been noticed?"

"Certainly, the town's in an uproar. A raging mob

has torn the courthouse down. We're running a fairly good picture of Wolfe, but we need a new one of you. Could you drop in at the studio, say in five minutes?"

"Sure, glad to. But I'm calling to settle a bet. Is there a warrant for us?"

"You're damn right there is. Judge Corbett signed it first thing after lunch. Look, Archie, let me send a man—"

I told him much obliged and hung up. If I hadn't spent that dime and learned there was a warrant, we wouldn't have taken any special precaution as we approached Saul's address on East Thirty-eighth Street and would have run smack into Sergeant Purley Stebbins, and the question of where to spend the night would have been taken off our hands.

It was nearly eight o'clock. Wolfe and I had each disposed of three orders of chili con carne at a little dump on 170th Street where a guy named Dixie knows how to make it, and I had made at least a dozen phone calls trying to get hold of Jimmy Donovan, Leonard Ashe's attorney. That might not have been difficult if I could have left word that Nero Wolfe had something urgent for him, and given a number for him to call, but that wouldn't have been practical, since an attorney is a sworn officer of the law, and he knew there was a warrant out for Wolfe, not to mention me. So I hadn't got him, and as we crawled with the traffic through East Thirty-eighth Street the sight of Wolfe's scowl in the rear-view mirror didn't make the scene any gayer.

My program was to let him out at Saul's address between Lexington and Third, find a place to park the car, and join him at Saul's. But just as I swung over and was braking I saw a familiar broad-shouldered figure on the sidewalk, switched from the brake to the gas pedal, and kept going. Luckily a gap had opened,

and the light was green at Third Avenue, so I rolled on
through, found a place to stop without blocking traffic,
and turned in the seat to tell Wolfe, "I came on by
because I decided we don't want to see Saul."

"You did." He was grim. "What flummery is this?"

"No flummery. Sergeant Purley Stebbins was just
turning in at the entrance. Thank God it's dark or he
would have seen us. Now where?"

"At the entrance of Saul's address?"

"Yes."

A short silence. "You're enjoying this," he said bitterly.

"I am like hell. I'm a fugitive from justice, and I
was going to spend the evening at the Polo Grounds
watching a ball game. Where now?"

"Confound it. You told Saul about Miss Weltz."

"Yes, sir. I told Fritz that if the Queen of Hearts
phones she is to call Saul's number, and I told Saul that
you'd rather have an hour alone with her than a blue
orchid. You know Saul."

Another silence. He broke it. "You have Mr. Donovan's home address."

"Right. East Seventy-seventh Street."

"How long will it take to drive there?"

"Ten minutes."

"Go ahead."

"Yes, sir. Sit back and relax." I fed gas.

It took only nine minutes at that time of evening,
and I found space to park right in the block, between
Madison and Park. As we walked to the number a cop
gave us a second glance, but Wolfe's size and carriage
rated that much notice without any special stimulation.
It was just my nerves. There were a canopy and a
doorman, and rugs in the lobby. I told the doorman
casually, "Donovan. We're expected," but he hung on.

"Yes, sir, but I have orders—Your name, please?"

"Judge Wolfe," Wolfe told him.

"One moment, please."

He disappeared through a door. It was more like five moments before he came back, looking questions but not asking them, and directed us to the elevator. Twelve B, he said.

Getting off at the twelfth floor, we didn't have to look for B because a door at the end of the foyer was standing open, and on the sill was Jimmy Donovan himself. In his shirt sleeves, with no necktie, he looked more like a janitor than a champion of the bar, and he sounded more like one when he blurted, "It's you, huh? What kind of a trick is this? *Judge* Wolfe!"

"No trick." Wolfe was courteous but curt. "I merely evaded vulgar curiosity. I had to see you."

"You can't see me. It's highly improper. You're a witness for the prosecution. Also a warrant has been issued for you, and I'll have to report this."

He was absolutely right. The only thing for him to do was shut the door on us and go to his phone and call the DA's office. My one guess why he didn't, which was all I needed, was that he would have given his shirt, and thrown in a necktie, to know what Wolfe was up to. He didn't shut the door.

"I'm not here," Wolfe said, "as a witness for the prosecution. I don't intend to discuss my testimony with you. As you know, your client, Leonard Ashe, came to me one day in July and wanted to hire me, and I refused. I have become aware of certain facts connected with what he told me that day which I think he should know about, and I want to tell him. I suppose it would be improper for me to tell you more than that, but it wouldn't be improper to tell him. He is on trial for first-degree murder."

I had the feeling I could see Donovan's brain working at it behind his eyes. "It's preposterous," he declared. "You know damn well you can't see him."

"I can if you'll arrange it. That's what I'm here for. You're his counsel. Early tomorrow morning will do, before the court sits. You may of course be present if you wish, but I suppose you would prefer not to. Twenty minutes with him will be enough."

Donovan was chewing his lip. "I can't ask you what you want to tell him."

"I understand that. I won't be on the witness stand, where you can cross-examine me, until tomorrow."

"No." The lawyer's eyes narrowed. "No, you won't. I can't arrange for you to see him; it's out of the question. I shouldn't be talking to you. It will be my duty to report this to Judge Corbett in the morning. Good evening, gentlemen."

He backed up and swung the door shut, but didn't bang it, which was gracious of him. We rang for the elevator, were taken down, and went out and back to the car.

"You'll phone Saul," Wolfe said.

"Yes, sir. His saying he'll report to the judge in the morning meant he didn't intend to phone the DA now, but he might change his mind. I'd rather move a few blocks before phoning."

"Very well. Do you know the address of Mrs. Leonard Ashe's apartment?"

"Yes, Seventy-third Street."

"Go in that direction. I have to see her, and you'd better phone and arrange it."

"You mean now."

"Yes."

"That should be a cinch. She's probably sitting

there hoping a couple of strange detectives will drop in. Do I have to be Judge Goodwin?"

"No. We are ourselves."

As I drove downtown on Park, and east on Seventy-fourth to Third Avenue, and down a block, and west on Seventy-third, I considered the approach to Robina Keane. By not specifying it Wolfe had left it to me, so it was my problem. I thought of a couple of fancy strategies, but by the time I got the car maneuvered to the curb in the only vacant spot between Lexington and Madison I had decided that the simplest was the best. After asking Wolfe if he had any suggestions and getting a no, I walked to Lexington and found a booth in a drugstore.

First I called Saul Panzer. There had been no word from the Queen of Hearts, but she had said around nine o'clock and it was only eight-forty. Sergeant Stebbins had been and gone. What he had said was that the police were concerned about the disappearance of Nero Wolfe because he was an important witness in a murder case, and they were afraid something might have happened to him, especially since Archie Goodwin was also gone. What he had not said was that Inspector Cramer suspected that Wolfe had tramped out of the courtroom hell-bent on messing the case up, and he wanted to get his hands on him quick. Had Wolfe communicated with Saul, and did Saul know where he was? There was a warrant out for both Wolfe and Goodwin. Saul had said no, naturally, and Purley had made some cutting remarks and left.

I dialed another number, and when a female voice answered I told it I would like to speak to Mrs. Ashe. It said Mrs. Ashe was resting and couldn't come to the phone. I said I was speaking for Nero Wolfe and it was urgent and vital. It said Mrs. Ashe absolutely would

not come to the phone. I asked it if it had ever heard of
Nero Wolfe, and it said of course. All right, I said, tell
Mrs. Ashe that he must see her immediately and he
can be there in five minutes. That's all I can tell you on
the phone, I said, except that if she doesn't see him
she'll never stop regretting it. The voice told me to
hold the wire, and was gone so long I began to wish I
had tried a fancy one, but just as I was reaching for the
handle of the booth door to let in some air it came back
and said Mrs. Ashe would see Mr. Wolfe. I asked it to
instruct the lobby guardians to admit us, hung up,
went out and back to the car, and told Wolfe, "Okay.
You'd better make it good after what I told her. No
word from Helen Weltz. Stebbins only asked some
foolish questions and got the answers he deserved."

He climbed out, and we walked to the number. This
one was smaller and more elegant, too elegant for
rugs. The doorman was practically Laurence Olivier,
and the elevator man was his older brother. They were
chilly but nothing personal. When we were let out at
the sixth floor the elevator man stayed at his open door
until we had pushed a button and the apartment door
had opened and we had been told to enter.

The woman admitting us wasn't practically Phyllis
Jay, she was Phyllis Jay. Having paid $4.40 or $5.50
several times to see her from an orchestra seat, I
would have appreciated this free close-up of her on a
better occasion, but my mind was occupied. So was
hers. Of course she was acting, since actresses always
are, but the glamour was turned off because the part
didn't call for it. She was playing a support for a friend
in need, and kept strictly in character as she relieved
Wolfe of his hat and cane and then escorted us into
a big living room, across it, and through an arch into a
smaller room.

Robina Keane was sitting on a couch, patting at her hair. Wolfe stopped three paces off and bowed. She looked up at him, shook her head as if to dislodge a fly, pressed her fingertips to her eyes, and looked at him again. Phyllis Jay said, "I'll be in the study, Robbie," waited precisely the right interval for a request to stay, didn't get it, and turned and went. Mrs. Ashe invited us to sit, and, after moving a chair around for Wolfe, I took one off at the side.

"I'm dead tired," she said. "I'm so empty, completely empty. I don't think I ever—But what is it? Of course it's something about my husband?"

Either the celebrated lilt of her voice was born in, or she had used it so much and so long that it might as well have been. She looked all in, no doubt of that, but the lilt was there.

"I'll make it as brief as I can," Wolfe told her. "Do you know that I have met your husband? That he called on me one day in July?"

"Yes, I know. I know all about it—now."

"It was to testify about our conversation that day that I was summoned to appear at his trial, by the State. In court this morning, waiting to be called, an idea came to me which I thought merited exploration, and if it was to bring any advantage to your husband the exploration could not wait. So I walked out, with Mr. Goodwin, my assistant, and we have spent the day on that idea."

"What idea?" Her hands were fists, on the couch for props.

"Later for that. We have made some progress, and we may make more tonight. Whether we do or not, I have information that will be of considerable value to your husband. It may not exculpate him, but at least it should raise sufficient doubt in the minds of the jury to get him acquitted. The problem is to get the information to the jury. It would take intricate and prolonged investigation to get it in the form of admissible evidence, and I have in mind a short cut. To take it I must have a talk with your husband."

"But he—How can you?"

"I must. I have just called on Mr. Donovan, his attorney, and asked him to arrange it, but I knew he wouldn't; that was merely to anticipate you. I knew that if I came to you, you would insist on consulting him, and I have already demonstrated the futility of that. I am in contempt of the court, and a warrant has been issued for my arrest. Also I am under subpoena as a witness for the prosecution, and it is improper for the defense counsel even to talk with me, let alone arrange an interview for me with his client. You, as the wife of a man on trial for his life, are under no such prescription. You have wide acquaintance and great personal charm. It would not be too difficult, certainly not impossible, for you to get permission to talk with your husband tomorrow morning before the court convenes; and you can take me with you. Twenty minutes would be ample, and even ten would do. Don't mention me in getting the permission; that's important; simply take me with you and we'll see. If it doesn't work there's another possible expedient. Will you do it?"

She was frowning. "I don't see—You just want to talk with him?"

"Yes."

"What do you want to tell him?"

"You'll hear it tomorrow morning when he does. It's complicated and conjectural. To tell you now might compromise my plan to get it to the jury, and I won't risk it."

"But tell me what it's about. Is it about me?"

Wolfe lifed his shoulders to take in a deep breath, and let them sag again. "You say you're dead tired, madam. So am I. I would be interested in you only if I thought you were implicated in the murder of Marie Willis, and I don't. At considerable risk to my reputation, my self-esteem, and possibly even my bodily freedom, I am undertaking a step which should be useful to your husband and am asking your help; but I am not asking you to risk anything. You have nothing to lose, but I have. Of course I have made an assumption that may not be valid: that, whether you are sincerely devoted to your husband or not, you don't want him convicted of murder. I can't guarantee that I have the key that will free him, but I'm not a novice in these matters."

Her jaw was working. "You didn't have to say that." The lilt was gone. "Whether I'm devoted to my husband. My husband's not a fool, but he acted like one. I love him very dearly, and I want—" Her jaw worked. "I love him very much. No, I don't want him convicted of murder. You're right, I have nothing to lose, nothing more to lose. But if I do this I'll have to tell Mr. Donovan."

"No. You must not. Not only would he forbid it, he would prevent it. This is for you alone."

She abandoned the prop of her fists and straightened her back. "I thought I was too tired to live," she said, lilting again, "and I am, but it's going to be a relief to do something." She left the couch and was on her feet. "I'm going to do it. As you say, I have a wide acquaintance, and I'll do it all right. You go on and make some more progress and leave this to me. Where can I reach you?"

Wolfe turned. "Saul's number, Archie."

I wrote it on a leaf of my notebook and went and

handed it to her. Wolfe arose. "I'll be there all night, Mrs. Ashe, up to nine in the morning, but I hope it will be before that."

I doubted if she heard him. Her mind was so glad to have a job that it had left us entirely. She did go with us to the foyer to see us out, but she wasn't there. I was barely across the threshold when she shut the door.

We went back to the car and headed downtown on Park Avenue. It seemed unlikely that Purley Stebbins had taken it into his head to pay Saul a second call, but a couple of blocks away I stopped to phone, and Saul said no, he was alone. It seemed even more unlikely that Stebbins had posted a man out front, but I stopped twenty yards short of the number and took a good long look. There was a curb space a little further down, and I squeezed the car into it and looked some more before opening the door for Wolfe to climb out. We crossed the street and entered the vestibule, and I pushed the button.

When we left the self-service elevator at the fifth floor Saul was there to greet us. I suppose to some people Saul Panzer is just a little guy with a big nose who always seems to need a shave, but to others, including Wolfe and me, he's the best free-for-all operative that ever tailed a subject. Wolfe had never been at his place before, but I had, many times over the years, mostly on Saturday nights with three or four others for some friendly and ferocious poker. Inside, Wolfe stood and looked around. It was a big room, lighted with two floor lamps and two table lamps. One wall had windows, another was solid with books, and the other two had pictures and shelves that were cluttered with everything from chunks of minerals to walrus tusks. In the far corner was a grand piano.

"A good room," Wolfe said. "Satisfactory. I congratulate you." He crossed to a chair, the nearest thing to his idea of a chair he had seen all day, and sat. "What time is it?"

"Twenty minutes to ten."

"Have you heard from that woman?"

"No, sir. Will you have some beer?"

"I will indeed. If you please."

In the next three hours he accounted for seven bottles. He also handled his share of liver pâté, herring, sturgeon, pickled mushrooms, Tunisian melon, and three kinds of cheese. Saul was certainly prancing as a host, though he is not a prancer. Naturally, the first time Wolfe ate under his roof, and possibly the last, he wanted to give him good grub, that was okay, but I thought the three kinds of cheese was piling it on a little. He sure would be sick of cheese by Saturday. He wasn't equipped to be so fancy about sleeping. Since he was the host it was his problem, and his arrangement was Wolfe in the bedroom, me on the couch in the big room, and him on the floor, which seemed reasonable.

However, at a quarter to one in the morning we were still up. Though time hadn't dragged too heavily, what with talking and eating and drinking and three hot games of checkers between Wolfe and Saul, all draws, we were all yawning. We hadn't turned in because we hadn't heard from Helen Weltz, and there was still a dim hope. The other thing was all set. Just after midnight Robina Keane had phoned and told Wolfe she had it fixed. He was to meet her in Room 917 at 100 Centre Street at half-past eight. He asked me if I knew what Room 917 was, and I didn't. After that came he leaned back in his chair and sat with his eyes closed for a while, then straightened up and told Saul he was ready for the third game of checkers.

At a quarter to one he left his chair, yawned and stretched, and announced, "Her panic wore off. I'm going to bed."

"I'm afraid," Saul apologized, "I have no pajamas you could get into, but I've got—"

The phone rang. I was nearest, and turned and got it. "This is Jackson four-three-one-oh-nine."

"I want— This is the Queen of Hearts."

"It sure is. I recognize your voice. This is Archie Goodwin. Where are you?"

"In a booth at Grand Central. I couldn't get rid of him, and then—but that doesn't matter now. Where are you?"

"In an apartment on Thirty-eighth Street with Mr. Wolfe, waiting for you. It's a short walk. I'll meet you at the information booth, upper level, in five minutes. Will you be there?"

"Yes."

"Sure?"

"Of course I will!"

I hung up, turned, and said loftily, "If it wore off it wore on again. Make some coffee, will you, Saul? She'll need either that or bourbon. And maybe she likes cheese."

I departed.

V

At six minutes past ten in the morning Assistant District Attorney Mandelbaum was standing at the end of his table in the courtroom to address Judge Corbett. The room was packed. The jury was in the box. Jimmy Donovan, defense attorney, looking not at all like a janitor, was fingering through some papers his assistant had handed him.

"Your Honor," Mandelbaum said, "I wish to call a witness whom I called yesterday, but he was not available. I learned only a few minutes ago that he is present. You will remember that on my application you issued a warrant for Mr. Nero Wolfe."

"Yes, I do." The judge cleared his throat. "Is he here?"

"He is." Mandelbaum turned and called, "Nero Wolfe!"

Having arrived at one minute to ten, we wouldn't have been able to get in if we hadn't pushed through to the officer at the door and told him who we were and that we were wanted. He had stared at Wolfe and admitted he recognized him, and let us in, and the attendant had managed to make room for us on a bench just as Judge Corbett entered. When Wolfe was called by Mandelbaum and got up to go forward I had enough space.

He walked down the aisle, through the gate, mounted the stand, turned to face the judge, and stood.

"I have some questions for you, Mr. Wolfe," the judge said, "after you are sworn."

The attendant extended the Book and administered the oath, and Wolfe sat. A witness-chair is supposed to take any size, but that one just barely made it.

The judge spoke. "You knew you were to be called yesterday. You were present, but you left and could not be found, and a warrant was issued for you. Are you represented by counsel?"

"No, sir."

"Why did you leave? You are under oath."

"I was impelled to leave by a motive which I thought imperative. I will of course expound it now if you so order, but I respectfully ask your indulgence. I understand that if my reason for leaving is unsatisfactory I will be in contempt of court and will suffer a penalty. But I ask, Your Honor, does it matter whether I am adjudged in contempt now, or later, after I have testified? Because my reason for leaving is inherent in my testimony, and therefore I would rather plead on the charge of contempt afterwards, if the court will permit. I'll still be here."

"Indeed you will. You're under arrest."

"No, I'm not."

"You're not under arrest?"

"No, sir. I came here voluntarily."

"Well, you are now." The judge turned his head. "Officer, this man is under arrest." He turned back. "Very well. You will answer to the contempt charge later. Proceed, Mr. Mandelbaum."

Mandelbaum approached the chair. "Please tell the jury your name, occupation, and address."

Wolfe turned to the jury box. "I am Nero Wolfe, a licensed private detective, with my office in my house at nine-eighteen West Thirty-fifth Street, Manhattan, New York City."

"Have you ever met the defendant in this case?" Mandelbaum pointed. "That gentleman."

"Yes, sir. Mr. Leonard Ashe."

"Where and under what circumstances did you meet him?"

"He called on me at my office, by appointment, at eleven o'clock in the morning of Tuesday, July thirteenth, this year."

"What did he say to you on that occasion?"

"That he wished to engage my professional services. That he had, the preceding day, arranged for an answering service for the telephone at his residence on

Seventy-third Street in New York. That he had learned, upon inquiry, that one of the employees of the answering service would be assigned to his number and would serve it five or six days a week. That he wanted to hire me to learn the identity of that employee, and to propose to her that she eavesdrop on calls made during the daytime to his number, and report on them either to him or to me—I can't say definitely which, because he wasn't clear on that point."

"Did he say why he wanted to make that arrangement?"

"No. He didn't get that far."

Donovan was up. "Objection, Your Honor. Conclusion of the witness as to the intention of the defendant."

"Strike it," Mandelbaum said amiably. "Strike all of his answer except the word 'No.' Your answer is 'No,' Mr. Wolfe?"

"Yes, sir."

"Did the defendant suggest any inducement to be offered to the employee to get her to do the eavesdropping?"

"He didn't name a sum, but he indicated that—"

"Not what he indicated. What he said."

I allowed myself a grin. Wolfe, who always insisted on precision, who loved to ride others, especially me, for loose talk, and who certainly knew the rules of evidence, had been caught twice. I promised myself to find occasion later to comment on it.

He was unruffled. "He said that he would make it worth her while, meaning the employee, but stated no amount."

"What else did he say?"

"That was about all. The entire conversation was

only a few minutes. As soon as I understand clearly what he wanted to hire me to do, I refused to do it."

"Did you tell him why you refused?"

"Yes, sir."

"What did you say?"

"I said that while it is the function of a detective to pry into people's affairs, I excluded from my field anything connected with marital difficulties and therefore declined his job."

"Had he told you that what he wanted was to spy on his wife?"

"No, sir."

"Then why did you mention marital difficulties to him?"

"Because I had concluded that that was the nature of his concern."

"What else did you say to him?"

Wolfe shifted in the chair. "I would like to be sure I understand the question. Do you mean what I said to him that day, or on a later occasion?"

"I mean that day. There was no later occasion, was there?"

"Yes, sir."

"Are you saying that you had another meeting with the defendant, on another day?"

"Yes, sir."

Mandelbaum held a pose. Since his back was to me I couldn't see his look of surprise, but I didn't have to. In his file was Wolfe's signed statement, saying among other things that he had not seen Leonard Ashe before or since July 13. His voice went up a notch. "When and where did this meeting take place?"

"Shortly after nine o'clock this morning, in this building."

"You met and spoke with the defendant in this building today?"

"Yes, sir."

"Under what circumstances?"

"His wife had arranged to see and speak with him, and she allowed me to accompany her."

"How did she arrange it? With whom?"

"I don't know."

"Was Mr. Donovan, the defense counsel, present?"

"No, sir."

"Who was?"

"Mrs. Ashe, Mr. Ashe, myself, and two armed guards, one at the door and one at the end of the room."

"What room was it?"

"I don't know. There was no number on the door. I think I could lead you to it."

Mandelbaum whirled around and looked at Robina Keane, seated on the front bench. Not being a lawyer, I didn't know whether he could get her to the stand or not. Of course a wife couldn't be summoned to testify against her husband, but I didn't know if this would have come under that ban. Anyway, he either skipped it or postponed it. He asked the judge to allow him a moment and went to the table to speak in an undertone to a colleague. I looked around. I had already spotted Guy Unger, in the middle of the audience on the left. Bella Velardi and Alice Hart were on the other side, next to the aisle. Apparently the Sixty-ninth Street office of Bagby Answers, Inc., was being womaned for the day from other offices. Clyde Bagby, the boss, was a couple of rows in front of Unger. Helen Weltz, the Queen of Hearts, whom I had driven from Saul's address to a hotel seven hours ago, was in the back, not far from me.

The colleague got up and left, in a hurry, and Mandelbaum went back to Wolfe.

"Don't you know," he demanded, "that it is a misdemeanor for a witness for the State to talk with the defendant charged with a felony?"

"No, sir, I don't. I understand it would depend on what was said. I didn't discuss my testimony with Mr. Ashe."

"What did you discuss?"

"Certain matters which I though would be of interest to him."

"What matters? Exactly what did you say?"

I took a deep breath, spread and stretched my fingers, and relaxed. The fat son-of-a-gun had put it over. Having asked that question, Mandelbaum couldn't possibly keep it from the jury unless Jimmy Donovan was a sap, and he wasn't.

Wolfe testified. "I said that yesterday, seated in this room awaiting your convenience, I had formed a surmise that certain questions raised by the murder of Marie Willis had not been sufficiently considered and investigated, and that therefore my role as a witness for the prosecution was an uncomfortable one. I said that I had determined to satisfy myself on certain points; that I knew that in leaving the courtroom I would become liable to a penalty for contempt of court, but that the integrity of justice was more important than my personal ease; that I had been confident that Judge Corbett would—"

"If you please, Mr. Wolfe. You are not now pleading to a charge of contempt."

"No, sir. You asked what I said to Mr. Ashe. He asked what surmise I had formed, and I told him—that it was a double surmise. First, that as one with long experience in the investigation of crime and culprits, I

had an appreciable doubt of his guilt. Second, that the
police had been so taken by the circumstances pointing
to Mr. Ashe—his obvious motive and his discovery of
the body—that their attention in other directions had
possibly been somewhat dulled. For example, an expe-
rienced investigator always has a special eye and ear
for any person occupying a privileged position. Such
persons are doctors, lawyers, trusted servants, inti-
mate friends, and, of course, close relatives. If one in
those categories is a rogue he has peculiar opportuni-
ties for his scoundrelism. It occurred to me that—"

"You said all this to Mr. Ashe?"

"Yes, sir. It occurred to me that a telephone-answering service was in the same kind of category as
those I have mentioned, as I sat in this room yesterday
and heard Mr. Bagby describe the operation of the
switchboards. An unscrupulous operator might, by listening in on conversations, obtain various kinds of information that could be turned to account—for
instance, about the stock market, about business or
professional plans, about a multitude of things. The
possibilities would be limitless. Certainly one, and perhaps the most promising, would be the discovery of
personal secrets. Most people are wary about discussing or disclosing vital secrets on the telephone, but
many are not, and in emergencies caution is often for-
gotten. It struck me that for getting the kind of information, or at least hints of it, that is most useful and
profitable for a blackmailer, a telephone-answering
service has potentialities equal to those of a doctor or
lawyer or trusted servant. Any operator at the switchboard could simply—"

"This is mere idle speculation, Mr. Wolfe. Did you
say all that to the defendant?"

"Yes, sir."

"How long were you with him?"

"Nearly half an hour. I can say a great deal in half an hour."

"No doubt. But the time of the court and jury should not be spent on irrelevancies." Mandelbaum treated the jury to one of his understanding glances, and went back to Wolfe. "You didn't discuss your testimony with the defendant?"

"No, sir."

"Did you make any suggestions to him regarding the conduct of his defense?"

"No, sir. I made no suggestions to him of any kind."

"Did you offer to make any kind of investigation for him as a contribution to his defense?"

"No, sir."

"Then why did you seek this interview with him?"

"One moment." Donovan was on his feet. "I submit, Your Honor, that this is the State's witness, and this is not proper direct examination. Surely it is cross-examination, and I object to it."

Judge Corbett nodded. "The objection is sustained. Mr. Mandelbaum, you know the rules of evidence."

"But I am confronted by an unforeseen contingency."

"He is still your witness. Examine him upon the merits."

"Also, Your Honor, he is in contempt."

"Not yet. That is in abeyance. Proceed."

Mandelbaum looked at Wolfe, glanced at the jury, went to the table and stood a moment gazing down at it, lifted his head, said, "No more questions," and sat down.

Jimmy Donovan arose and stepped forward, but addressed the bench instead of the witness-stand. "Your Honor, I wish to state that I knew nothing of the meeting this morning, of the witness with my client, either before or after it took place. I only learned of it here and now. If you think it desirable, I will take the stand to be questioned about it under oath."

Judge Corbett shook his head. "I don't think so, Mr. Donovan. Not unless developments suggest it."

"At any time, of course." Donovan turned. "Mr. Wolfe, why did you seek an interview this morning with Mr. Ashe?"

Wolfe was relaxed but not smug. "Because I had acquired information which cast a reasonable doubt on his guilt, and I wanted to get it before the court and the jury without delay. As a witness for the prosecution, with a warrant out for my arrest, I was in a difficult situation. It occurred to me that if I saw and talked with Mr. Ashe the fact would probably be disclosed in the course of my examination by Mr. Mandelbaum; and if so, he would almost certainly ask me what had been said. Therefore I wanted to tell Mr. Ashe what I had surmised and what I had discovered. If Mr. Mandelbaum allowed me to tell all I had said to Mr. Ashe, that would do it. If he dismissed me before I finished, I thought it likely that on cross-examination the defense attorney would give me an opportunity to go on." He turned a palm up. "So I sought an interview with Mr. Ashe."

The judge was frowning. One of the jurors made a noise, and the others looked at him. The audience stirred, and someone tittered. I was thinking Wolfe had one hell of a nerve, but he hadn't violated any law I had ever heard of, and Donovan had asked him a plain question and got a plain answer. I would have given a ream of foolscap to see Donovan's face.

If his face showed any reaction to the suggestion

given him, his voice didn't. "Did you say more to Mr. Ashe than you have already testified to?"

"Yes, sir."

"Please tell the jury what you said to him."

"I said that I left this room yesterday morning, deliberately risking a penalty for contempt of court, to explore my surmises. I said that, taking my assistant, Mr. Archie Goodwin, with me, I went to the office of Bagby Answers, Incorporated, on Sixty-ninth Street, where Marie Willis was murdered. I said that from a look at the switchboards I concluded that it would be impossible for any one operator—"

Mandelbaum was up. "Objection, Your Honor. Conclusions of the witness are not admissible."

"He is merely relating," Donovan submitted, "what he said to Mr. Ashe. The Assistant District Attorney asked him to."

"The objection is overruled," Judge Corbett said dryly.

Wolfe resumed. "I said I had concluded that it would be impossible for any one operator to eavesdrop frequently on her lines without the others becoming aware of it, and therefore it must be done collusively if at all. I said that I had spoken at some length with two of the operators, Alice Hart and Bella Velardi, who had been working and living there along with Marie Willis, and had received two encouragements for my surmise: one, that they were visibly disturbed at my declared intention of investigating them fully and ruthlessly, and tolerated my rudeness beyond reason; and two, that it was evident that their personal expenditures greatly exceeded their salaries. I said—may I ask, sir, is it necessary for me to go on repeating that phrase, 'I said'?"

"I think not," Donovan told him. "Not if you confine

yourself strictly to what you said to Mr. Ashe this morning."

"I shall do so. The extravagance in personal expenditures was true also of the third operator who had lived and worked there with Marie Willis, Helen Weltz. It was her day off, and Mr. Goodwin and I drove to her place in the country, near Katonah in Westchester County. She was more disturbed even than the other two; she was almost hysterical. With her was a man named Guy Unger, and he too was disturbed. After I had stated my intention to investigate everyone connected with Bagby Answers, Incorporated, he asked to speak with me privately and offered me ten thousand dollars for services which he did not specify. I gathered that he was trying to bribe me to keep my hands off, and I declined the offer."

"You said all that to Mr. Ashe?"

"Yes, sir. Meanwhile Helen Weltz had spoken privately with Mr. Goodwin, and had told him she wanted to speak with me, but must first get rid of Mr. Unger. She said she would phone my office later. Back in the city, I dared not go to my home, since I was subject to arrest and detention, so Mr. Goodwin and I went to the home of a friend, and Helen Weltz came to us there sometime after midnight. My attack had broken her completely, and she was in terror. She confessed that for years the operation had been used precisely as I had surmised. All of the switchboard operators had been parties to it, including Marie Willis. Their dean, Alice Hart, collected information—"

There was an interruption. Alice Hart, on the aisle, with Bella Velardi next to her, got up and headed for the door, and Bella followed her. Eyes went to them from all directions, including Judge Corbett's, but nobody said or did anything, and when they were five steps from the door I sang out to the guard, "That's Alice Hart in front!"

He blocked them off. Judge Corbett called, "Officer, no one is to leave the room!"

The audience stirred and muttered, and some stood up. The judge banged his gavel and demanded order, but he couldn't very well threaten to have the room cleared. Miss Hart and Miss Velardi gave it up and went back to their seats.

When the room was still the judge spoke to Wolfe. "Go ahead."

He did so. "Alice Hart collected information from them and gave them cash from time to time, in addition to their salaries. Guy Unger and Clyde Bagby also gave them cash occasionally. The largest single amount ever received by Helen Weltz was fifteen hundred dollars, given her about a year ago by Guy Unger. In three years she received a total of approximately fifteen thousand dollars, not counting her salary. She didn't know what use was made of the information she passed on to Alice Hart. She wouldn't admit that she had knowledge that any of it had been used for blackmailing, but she did admit that some of it could have been so used."

"Do you know," Judge Corbett asked him, "where Helen Weltz is now?"

"Yes, sir. She is present. I told her that if she came and faced it the District Attorney might show appreciation for her help."

"Have you anything to add that you told Mr. Ashe this morning?"

"I have, Your Honor. Do you wish me to differentiate clearly between what Helen Weltz told me and my own exposition?"

"No. Anything whatever that you said to Mr. Ashe."

"I told him that the fact that he had tried to hire me to learn the identity of the Bagby operator who would service his number, and to bribe her to eavesdrop on his line, was one of the points that had caused me to doubt his guilt; that I had questioned whether a man who was reluctant to undertake such a chore for himself would be likely to strangle the life out of a woman and then open a window and yell for the police. Also I asked him about the man who telephoned him to say that if Ashe would meet him at the Bagby office on Sixty-ninth Street he thought they could talk Miss Willis out of it. I asked if it was possible that the voice was Bagby's, and Ashe said it was quite possible, but if so he had disguised his voice."

"Had you any evidence that Mr. Bagby made that phone call?"

"No, Your Honor. All I had, besides my assumptions from known facts and my own observations, was what Miss Weltz had told me. One thing she had told me was that Marie Willis had become an imminent threat to the whole conspiracy. She had been ordered by both Unger and Bagby to accept Ashe's proposal to eavesdrop on his line, and not to tell Mrs. Ashe, whom Miss Willis idolized; and she had refused and announced that she was going to quit. Of course that made her an intolerable peril to everyone concerned. The success and security of the operation hinged on the fact that no victim ever had any reason to suspect that Bagby Answers, Incorporated, was responsible for his distress. It was Bagby who got the information, but it was Unger who used it, and the tormented under the screw could not know where the tormentor had got the screw. So Miss Willis's rebellion and decision to quit—combined, according to Miss Weltz, with an implied threat to expose the whole business—were a mortal menace to any and all of them, ample provocation for murder to one willing to risk that extreme. I told Mr. Ashe that all this certainly established a reasonable doubt of his guilt, but I also went beyond that and considered briefly the most likely candidate to replace him. Do you wish that too?"

The judge was intent on him. "Yes. Proceed."

"I told Mr. Ashe that I greatly preferred Mr. Bagby. The mutual alibi of Miss Hart and Miss Velardi might be successfully impeached, but they have it, and besides I have seen and talked with them and was not impressed. I exclude Miss Weltz because when she came to me last evening she had been jolted by consternation into utter candor, or I am a witless gull; and that excludes Mr. Unger too, because Miss Weltz claims certain knowledge that he was on his boat in the Sound all of that evening. As for Mr. Bagby, he had most at stake. He admits that he went to his apartment around the time of the murder, and his apartment is on Seventieth Street, not far from where the murder occurred. I leave the timetable to the police; they are extremely efficient with timetables. Regarding the telephone call, Mr. Ashe said it could have been his voice."

Wolfe pursed his lips. "I think that's all—no, I also told Mr. Ashe that this morning I sent a man, Saul Panzer, to keep an eye on Mr. Bagby's office in Forty-seventh Street, to see that no records are removed or destroyed. I believe that covers it adequately, Your Honor. I would now like to plead to the charge of contempt, both on behalf of Mr. Goodwin and of myself. If I may—"

"No." Judge Corbett was curt. "You know quite

well you have made that charge frivolous by the situation you have created. The charge is dismissed. Are you through with the witness, Mr. Donovan?"

"Yes, Your Honor. No more questions."

"Mr. Mandelbaum?"

The Assistant District Attorney got up and approached the bench. "Your Honor will appreciate that I find myself in an extraordinary predicament." He sounded like a man with a major grievance. "I feel that I am entitled to ask for a recess until the afternoon session, to consider the situation and consult with my colleagues. If my request is granted, I also ask that I be given time, before the recess is called, to arrange for five persons in the room to be taken into custody as material witnesses—Alice Hart, Bella Velardi, Helen Weltz, Guy Unger, and Clyde Bagby."

"Very well." The judge raised his eyes and his voice. "The five persons just named will come forward. The rest of you will keep your seats and preserve order."

All of them obeyed but two. Nero Wolfe left the witness chair and stepped down to the floor, and as he did so Robina Keane sprang up from her place on the front bench, ran to him, threw her arms around his neck, and pressed her cheek against his. As I said before, actresses always act, but I admit that was unrehearsed and may have been artless. In any case, I thoroughly approved, since it indicated that the Ashe family would prove to be properly grateful, which after all was the main point.

VI

The thought may have occurred to you, that's all very nice, and no doubt Ashe sent a handsome check, but after all one reason Wolfe walked out was because he hated to sit against a perfumed woman on a wooden bench waiting for his turn to testify, and he had to do it all over again when the State was ready with its case, against the real murderer. It did look for a while as if he might have to face up to that, but a week before the trial opened he was informed that he wouldn't be needed, and he wasn't. They had plenty without him to persuade a jury to bring in a verdict of guilty against Clyde Bagby.

When a
Man Murders . . .

I

"That's just it," she declared, trying to keep her voice steady. "We're not actually married."

My brows went up. Many a time, seated there at my desk in Nero Wolfe's office, I have put the eye on a female visitor to estimate how many sound reasons she might offer why a wedding ring would be a good buy, but usually I don't bother with those who are already hitched, so my survey of this specimen had been purely professional, especially since her husband was along. Now, however, I changed focus. She would unquestionably grade high, after allowing for the crease in her forehead, the redness around her eyes, and the tension of her jaw muscles, tightening her lips. Making such allowances was nothing new for me, since most of the callers at that office are in trouble, seldom trivial.

Wolfe, who had just come down from the plant rooms in the roof and got his impressive bulk settled in his oversized chair behind his desk, glared at her. "But you told Mr. Goodwin—" he began, stopped, and turned to me. "Archie?"

I nodded. "Yes, sir. A man on the phone said his

name was Paul Aubry, and he and his wife wanted to come to see you as soon as possible, and I told him six o'clock. I didn't tell him to bring their marriage certificate."

"We have one," she said, "but it's no good." She twisted her head around and up. "Tell him, Paul."

She was in the red leather chair near the end of Wolfe's desk. It is roomy, with big arms, and Paul Aubry was perched on one of them, with an arm extended along the top of the back. I had offered him one of the yellow chairs, which are perfectly adequate, but apparently he preferred to stick closer to his wife, if any.

"It's one hell of a mess!" he blurted.

He wasn't red-eyed, but there was evidence that he was sharing the trouble. His hand on top of the chairback was tightened into a fist, his fairly well-arranged face was grim, and his broad shoulders seemed to be hunched in readiness to meet an attack. He bent his head to meet her upward look.

"Don't you want to tell him?" he asked.

She shook her head. "No, you." She put out a hand to touch his knee and then jerked it away.

His eyes went to Wolfe. "We were married six months ago—six months and four days—but now we're not married, according to the law. We're not married because my wife, Caroline—" He paused to look down at her, and, his train of thought interrupted, reached to take her hand, but it moved, and he didn't get it.

He stood up, squared his shoulders, faced Wolfe, and spoke faster and louder. "Four years ago she married a man named Sidney Karnow. A year later he enlisted in the Army and was sent to Korea. A few months later she was officially informed that he was dead—killed in action. A year after that I met her and fell in love with her and asked her to marry me, but she wouldn't until two years had passed since Karnow died, and then she did. Three weeks ago Karnow turned up alive—he phoned his lawyer here from San Francisco—and last week he got his Army discharge, and Sunday, day before yesterday, he came to New York."

Aubry hunched his shoulders like Jack Dempsey ready to move in. "I'm not giving her up," he told the world. "I—will—not—give—her—up!"

Wolfe grunted. "It's fifteen million to one, Mr. Aubry."

"What do you mean, fifteen million?"

"The People of the State of New York. They're lined up against you, officially at least, I'm one of them. Why in heaven's name did you come to me? You should have cleared out with her days ago—Turkey, Australia, Burma, anywhere—if she was willing. It may not be too late if you hurry. Bon voyage."

Aubry stood a moment, took a deep breath, turned and went to the yellow chair I had placed, and sat. Becoming aware that his fists were clenched, he opened them, cupped his hands on his knees, and looked at Caroline. He lifted a hand and let it fall back to his knee. "I can't touch you," he said.

"No," she said. "Not while—no."

"Okay, you tell him. He might think I was bulling it. You tell him."

She shook her head. "He can ask me. I'm right here. Go ahead."

He went to Wolfe. "It's like this. Karnow was an only child, and his parents are both dead, and he inherited a pile, nearly two million dollars. He left a will giving half of it to my—to Caroline, and the other half to some relatives, an aunt and a couple of cousins. His lawyer had the will. After notice of his death came it took several months to get the will probated and the estate distributed, on account of special formalities in a case like that. Caroline's share was a little over nine hundred thousand dollars, and she had it when I met her, and was living on the income. All I had was a job selling automobiles, making around a hundred and fifty a week, but it was her I fell in love with, not the million, just for your information. When we got married it was her idea that I ought to buy an agency, but I'm not saying I fought it. I shopped around and we bought a good one at a bargain, and—"

"What kind of agency?"

"Automobile." Aubry's tone implied that that was the only kind of agency worth mentioning. "Brandon and Hiawatha. It took nearly half of Caroline's capital to swing it, but in the past three months we've cleared over twenty thousand after taxes, and the future was looking rosy—when this happened. I was figuring—but to hell with that, that's sunk. This proposition we want to offer Karnow, it's not my idea and it's not Caroline's, it's ours. It just came out of all our talking and talking after we heard Karnow was alive. Last week we went to Karnow's lawyer, Jim Beebe, to get him to propose it to Karnow, but we couldn't persuade him. He said he knew Karnow too well—he was in college with him—and he knew Karnow wouldn't even listen to it. So we decided—"

"What was the proposal?"

"We thought it was a fair offer. We offered to turn it all over to him, the half-million Caroline has left, and the agency, the whole works, if he would consent to a divorce. Also I would continue to run the agency if he wanted to hire me. Also Caroline would ask for no settlement and no alimony."

"It was my idea," she said.

"It was ours," he insisted.

Wolfe was frowning at them. My brows were up again. Evidently he really was in love with her and not the dough, and I'm all for true love up to a point. As for her, my attitude flopped back to the purely professional. Granting that she was set to ditch her lawful husband, if she felt that her Paul was worth a million bucks to her it would have taken too much time and energy to try to talk her out of it. Cocking an eye at his earnest phiz, which was passable, but no pin-up, I would have said that she was overpricing him.

He was going on. "So when Beebe wouldn't do it and we learned that Karnow had come to New York, we decided I would see him myself and put it up to him. We only decided that last night. I had some business appointments this morning, and this afternoon I went to his hotel—he's at the Churchill—and went up to his room. I didn't phone ahead because I've never seen him, and I wanted to see him before I spoke with him. I wanted a look at him."

Aubry stopped to rub a palm across his forehead, pressing hard. When his hand dropped to his thigh it became a fist again. "One trouble," he said, "was that I wasn't absolutely sure what I was going to say. The main proposition, that was all right, but there were two other things in my mind. The agency is incorporated, and half of the stock is in Caroline's name and half in mine. Well, I could tell him that if he didn't take the offer I would hang on to my half and fight for it, but I hadn't decided whether to or not. The other thing, I could tell him that Caroline is pregnant. It wouldn't have been true, and I guess I wouldn't have said it, but it was in my mind. Anyhow it doesn't matter because I didn't see him."

He clamped his jaw and then relaxed it. "This is where I didn't shine, I admit that, but it wasn't just cold feet. I went up to the door of his room, twenty-three-eighteen, without phoning, and I lifted my hand to knock, but I didn't. Because I realized I was trembling, I was trembling all over. I stood there a while to calm down, but I didn't calm. I realized that if I went in there and put it to him and he said nothing doing, there was no telling what might happen. The way I was feeling I was a lot more apt to queer it than help it. So I just ducked it. I'm not proud of it, but I'm telling you, I gave it a miss and came away. Caroline was waiting for me in a bar down the street, and I went and told her, and that wasn't easy either, telling her I had muffed it. Up to then she had thought I could handle about anything that came along. She thought I was good."

"I still do, Paul," she told him.

"Yeah? I can't touch you."

"Not now. Not until—" Her hand fluttered. "Don't keep saying that."

"Okay, we'll skip it." He went back to Wolfe. "So I told her the man-to-man approach was a bum idea, and we sat and chewed at it. We decided that none of our friends was up to it. The lawyer I use for the agency wouldn't be worth a damn. When one of us thought of you—I forget which—it clicked with both of us, and I went to a booth to phone for an appointment. Maybe you can get him down here and you make him the proposition yourself, or if he won't come you can send Archie Goodwin to see him. Caroline has the idea it might be better to send Goodwin because Karnow's thin-skinned and you might irritate him. We'll leave that to you. I wish I could say if you get him to take our offer you can write your own ticket, any amount you want to make it, but in that case we won't be any too flush so I have to mention it. Five thousand dollars, something like that, we could manage that all right. But for God's sake go to it—now, today, tonight!"

Wolfe cleared his throat. "I'm not a lawyer, Mr. Aubry, I'm a detective."

"I know that, but what's the difference? You have a reputation for getting things out of people. We want you to detect a way of getting Karnow to accept our proposition."

Wolfe grunted. "I could challenge your diction, but you're in no mood to debate semantics. And my fees are based on the kind and amount of work done. Your job seems fairly simple. In describing it to me, how candid have you been?"

"Completely. Absolutely."

"Nonsense. Complete candor is beyond the reach of man or woman. If Mr. Karnow accepts your proposal, can I rely on you to adhere to its terms as you have stated them?"

"Yes. You're damn right you can."

Wolfe's head turned. "Mrs. Karnow, are you—"

"She's not Mrs. Karnow!" Aubrey barked. "She's my wife!"

Wolfe's shoulders went up half an inch and dropped back. "Madam, are you sure you understand the proposal and will faithfully adhere to it?"

"Yes," she said firmly.

"You know that you will be relinquishing a dower right, a legal right, in a large property?"

"Yes."

"Then I must ask a few questions about Mr. Karnow—of you, since Mr. Aubry has never met him. You had no child by him?"

"No."

"You were in love when you married, presumably?"

"We thought—I guess we were. Yes, say we were."

"Did it cool off?"

"Not exactly." She hesitated, deciding how to put it. "Sidney was sensitive and high-strung—you see. I still say 'was' because for so long I thought he was dead. I was only nineteen when we were married, and I suppose I didn't know how to take him. He enlisted in the Army because he thought he ought to, because he hadn't been in the World War and he thought he should do his share of peeling potatoes—that was how he put it—but I didn't agree with him. I had found out by then that what I thought wasn't very important, nor what I felt either. If you're going to try to get him to agree to this of course you want to know what he's like, but I don't really know myself, not after all this time. Maybe it would help for you to read the letters I got from him after he enlisted. He only sent me three, one from Camp Givens and two from Korea—he didn't like writing letters. My husb—Paul said I should bring them along to show you."

She opened her bag, fished in it, and produced some sheets of paper clipped together. I went to get them and hand them to Wolfe, and, since I would probably be elected to deliver the proposal, I planted myself at his elbow and read along with him. All three letters are still in the archives in our office, but I'll present only one, the last one, to give you a sample of the tone and style:

Dear Carrie my true and loving mate I hope:

Pardon me, but my weakness is showing. I would like to be where you are this minute and tell you why I didn't like your new dress, and you would go and put on another one, and we would go to Chambord and eat snails and drink Richebourg and then go to the Velvet Yoke and eat lady fingers and drink tomato soup, and then we would go home and take hot baths and go to sleep on fine linen sheets spread over mattresses three feet thick, covered with an electric blanket. After several days of that I would begin to recognize myself and would put my arms around you and we would drown in delight.

Now I suppose I should tell you enough about this place to make you understand why I would rather be somewhere else, but that would be too easy to bother with, and anyway, as you well know, I hate to write, and especially I hate to try to write what I feel. Since the time is getting closer and closer when I'll try to kill somebody and probably succeed, I've been going through my memory for things about death. Herodotus said, "Death is a delightful hiding-place for weary men." Epictetus said, "What is death but a bugbear?" Montaigne said, "The deadest deaths are the best." I'll quote those to the man I'm going to kill and then he won't mind so much.

Speaking of death, if he should get me instead of me getting him, something I did before I left New York will give you quite a shock. I wish I could be around to see how you take it. You claim you have never worried about money, that it's not worth it. Also you've told me that I always talk sardonic but haven't got it in me to act sardonic. This will show you. I'll admit I have to die to get the last laugh, but that will be sardonic too. I wonder do I love you or hate you? They're hard to tell apart. Remember me in thy dreams.

> Your sardonic
> Kavalier Karnow

As I went to my desk to put the letters under a paperweight Caroline was speaking. "I wrote him two long letters every week. I must have sent him over fifty letters, and he never mentioned them the few times he wrote. I want to try to be fair to him, but he always said he was egocentric, and I guess he was."

"Not was," Aubry said grimly. "*Is*. He *is*." He asked Wolfe, "Doesn't that letter prove he's a nut?"

"He is—uh—picturesque," Wolfe conceded. He turned to Caroline. "What had he done before he left New York that—upon his death—gave you quite a shock?"

She shook her head. "I don't know. Naturally I thought he had changed his will and left me out. After word came that he was dead I showed that letter to the lawyer, Jim Beebe, and told him what I thought, and he said it did sound like it, but there had been no change made in the will as far as he knew, and Sidney must have been stringing me."

"Not too adroitly," Wolfe objected. "It isn't so simple to disinherit a wife. However, since he didn't try— What do you know about the false report of his death?"

"Only a little from an item in the paper," she said, "but Jim Beebe told me some more. He was left for dead in the field in a retreat, but actually he was only stunned, and he was taken prisoner. He was a prisoner for nearly two years, and then he escaped across the Yalu River, and then he was in Manchuria. By that time he could talk their language—he was wonderful

with languages—and he made friends in a village and
wore their clothes, and it seems—I'm not sure about
this, but apparently he was converted to communism."

"Then he's a jackass," Wolfe asserted.

"Oh, no, he's not a jackass." She was positive.
"Maybe he was just being picturesque. Anyhow, a few
months after the truce was signed and the fighting
stopped he finally decided he had had enough of it and
went back across the Yalu and made his way to South
Korea and reported to an army post, and they sent him
home. And now he's here," She stretched her hands
out, at arm's length. "Please, Mr. Wolfe? Please?"

Though of course she didn't know it, that was bad
tactics. Wolfe's reaction to an emotional appeal from a
man is rarely favorable, and from a woman, never. He
turned away from the painful sight, to me. "Archie.
You're in my hire, and I can dispatch you on errands
within the scope of my métier, but this one isn't. Are
you willing to tackle it?"

He was being polite. What he really meant was:
Five grand will pay a lot of salaries, including yours,
and you will please proceed to earn it for me. So, wishing to be polite too, I suggested a compromise. "I'm
willing to go get him and bring him here, and you can
tackle it."

"No," he said flatly. "Regarding the proposal as
quixotic, as I do, I would be a feeble advocate. I aban-
don it to your decision."

"I deeply appreciate it," I assured him. "Nuts. If I
say no I won't hear the last of it for months, so I'll
meet you all the way and say yes. I'll take a shot at it."

"Very well. We'll discuss it after dinner, and in the
morning you can—"

They drowned him out, both of them cutting in to
protest. They couldn't wait until tomorrow, they had to

know. They protested to him and then appealed to me. Why put it off? Why not now? I do not react to emotional appeals the way Wolfe does, and I calmed them down by agreeing with them.

"Very well," Wolfe acquiesced, which was noble of him. "But you must have with you the proposal in writing, in duplicate, signed by Mr. Aubry and—uh—you, madam. You must sign it as Caroline Karnow. Archie. At the bottom, on the left, type the word 'accepted' and a colon. Under the circumstances he would be a nincompoop not to sign it, but it would probably be imprudent to tell him so. Your notebook, please?"

I swiveled and got it from the drawer.

II

I rapped with my knuckles, smartly but not aggressively, on the door of Room 2318 on the twenty-third floor of the Hotel Churchill.

The clients had wanted to camp in Wolfe's office to await word from me, but I had insisted they should be as handy as possible in case developments called for their personal appearance, and they were downstairs in the Tulip Bar, not, I hoped, proceeding to get lit. People in serious trouble have a tendency to eat too little or drink too much, or both.

I knocked again, louder and longer.

On the way in the taxi I had collected a little more information about Sidney Karnow, at least as he had been three years back. His attitude toward money had been somewhat superior, but he had shown no inclination to scatter his pile around regardless. So far as Caroline knew, he hadn't scattered it at all. He had been more than decent about meeting her modest re-

quirements, and even anticipating them. That gave me
no lead, but other details did. The key words were
"egocentric," which was bad, and "proud," which was
good. If he really had pride and wasn't just using it as
a cover for something that wouldn't stand daylight,
fine. No proud man would want to eat his breakfasts
with a woman who was eager to cough up nearly a
million bucks for the privilege of eating them with another guy. That, I had decided, was the line to take,
but I would have to go easy on the wording until I had
sized him up.

Evidently the sizing up would be delayed, since my
knocking got no response. Not wanting to risk a picturesque refusal to make an appointment, I hadn't phoned
ahead. I decided to go down and tell the clients that
patience would be required for ten minutes or ten
hours, and take on a sandwich and a glass of milk and
then come up for another try, but before I turned away
my hand went automatically to the knob for a twist
and a push, and the door opened. I stood a second, then
pushed it a foot farther, stuck my head in, and called,
"Mr. Karnow! Karnow!"

No answer. I swung the door open and crossed the
sill. Beyond the light I was letting in was darkness,
and I would probably have backed out and shut the
door and beat it if I hadn't had such a good nose. When
it told me there was a faint odor that I should recognize, and a couple of sniffs confirmed it, I found the
wall switch and flipped it, and moved on in. A man was
there, spread-eagled on the floor near an open door,
flat on his back.

I took a step toward him—that was involuntary—
then wheeled and went and closed the door to the hall,
and returned. At a glance, from the description Caroline had given me, it was Sidney Karnow. He was

dressed, but without a jacket or tie. I squatted and slipped a hand inside his shirt and held my breath; nothing doing. I picked a few fibers from the rug and put them over his nostrils; they didn't move. I got the lashes of his right eye between finger and thumb and pulled the lid partly down; it came stiffly and didn't want to go back. I lifted his hand and pressed hard on the fingernail, and then removed the pressure; it stayed white. Actually I was overdoing it, because the temperature of the skin of his chest had been enough.

I stood up and looked down at him. It was unquestionably Karnow. I looked at my wristwatch and saw 7:22. Through the open door beyond him I could see the glitter of bathroom tiles and fittings, and, detouring around his outstretched arm, I went and squatted again for a close-up of two objects on the floor. One was a GI sidearm, a .45. I didn't touch it. The other was a big wad of bathtowels, and I touched it enough to learn, from a scorched hole and powder black, that it had been used to muffle the gun. I had seen no sign on the body of a bullet's entrance or exit, and to find it I would have had to turn him over, and what did it matter? I got erect and shut my eyes to think. It is my habit, long established, when I open doors where I haven't been invited, to avoid touching the knob with my fingertips. Had I followed it this time? I decided yes. Also, had I flipped the light switch with my knuckle? Again yes. Had I made prints anywhere else? No.

I crossed to the switch and used my knuckle again, got out my handkerchief to open the door and pull it shut after me, took an elevator down to the lobby floor, found a phone booth and dialed a number. The voice that answered belonged to Fritz. I told him I wanted Wolfe.

He was shocked. "But Archie, he's at dinner!"

"Yeah, I know. Tell him I've been trapped by cannibals and they're slicing me, and step on it."

It was a full two minutes before Wolfe's outraged voice came. "Well, Archie?"

"No, sir. Not well. I'm calling from a booth in the Churchill lobby. I left the clients in the bar, went up to Karnow's room, found the door unlocked, and entered. Karnow was on the floor, dead, shot with an army gun. The gun's there, but it wasn't suicide, the gun was muffled with a wad of towels. How do I earn that five grand now?"

"Confound it, in the middle of a meal."

If you think that was put on, you're wrong. I know that damn fat genius. That was how he felt, and he said it, that's all.

I ignored it. "I left nothing in the room," I told him, "and I had no audience, so we're fancy free. I know it's hard to talk with your mouth full, but—"

"Shut up." Silence for four seconds, then: "Did he die within the past ninety minutes?"

"No. The skin on his chest has started to cool off."

"Did you see anything suggestive?"

"No. I was in there maybe three minutes. I wanted to interrupt your dinner. I can go back and give it a whirl."

"Don't." He was curt. "There's nothing to be gained by deferring the discovery. I'll have Fritz notify the police anonymously. Bring Mr. Aubry and Mrs. Karnow—have they eaten?"

"They may be eating now. I told them to."

"See that they eat, and then bring them here on a pretext. Devise one."

"Don't tell them?"

"No. I'll tell them. Have them here in an hour and

ten minutes, not sooner. I've barely started my dinner
—and now this."

He hung up.

After crossing the lobby and proceeding along one
of the long, wide, and luxurious corridors, near the entrance to the Tulip Bar I was stopped by an old acquaintance, Tim Evarts, the first assistant house dick,
only they don't call him that, of the Churchill. He
wanted to chin, but I eased him off. If he had known
that I had just found a corpse in one of his rooms and
forgot to mention it, he wouldn't have been so
chummy.

The big room was only half filled with customers at
that hour. The clients were at a table over in a corner,
and as I approached and Aubry got up to move a chair
for me I gave them both a mark for good conduct. Presumably they were on the sharpest edge of anxiety to
hear what I was bringing, but they didn't yap or claw
at me.

When I was seated I spoke to their waiting faces.
"No answer to my knock. I'll have to try again. Meanwhile let's eat."

I couldn't see that their disappointment was anything but plain, wholesome disappointment.

"I can't eat now," Caroline said wearily.

"I strongly advise it," I told her. "I don't mean a
major meal, but something like a piece of melon and a
sturgeon sandwich? We can get that here. Then I'll try
again, and if there's still no answer we'll see. You can't
stick around here all night."

"He might show up any minute," Aubry suggested.
"Or he might come in and leave again. Wouldn't it be
better if you stayed up there?"

"Not on an empty stomach." I was firm. "And I'll
bet Mrs.— What do I call you?"

"Oh, call me Caroline."

"I'll bet you haven't eaten for a week. You may need some energy, so you'd better refuel."

That was a tough half-hour. She did eat a little, and Aubry cleaned up a turkey sandwich and a hunk of cheese, but she was having a hard time to keep from showing that she thought I was a cold-blooded pig, and Aubry, as the minutes went by, left no doubt of his attitude. It was pretty gloomy. When my coffee cup was empty I told them to sit tight, got up and went out and down the corridor to the men's room, locked myself in a cubicle against the chance that Aubry might appear, and stayed there a quarter of an hour. Then I returned to the bar and went to their table and told them, "No answer. I phoned Mr. Wolfe, and he has an idea and wants to see us right away. Let's go."

"No," Caroline said.

"What for? Aubry demanded.

"Look," I said, "when Mr. Wolfe has an idea and wants me to hear it, I oblige him. So I'm going. You can stay here and soak in the agony, or you can come along. Take your pick."

From their expressions it was a good guess that they were beginning to think that Wolfe was a phony and I was a slob, but since their only alternative was to call the deal off and start hunting another salesman for their line, they had to string along. After Aubry paid the check we left, and in the corridor I steered them to the left and around to an exit on a side street, to avoid the main lobby, because by that time some city employees had certainly responded to Fritz's anonymous phone call to headquarters, and from remarks they had made I had learned that the Aubrys were known at the Churchill. The doorman who waved up a taxi for us called them by name.

At the house I let us in with my key, and, closing the door, shot the chain bolt. As I escorted them down the hall to the office a glance at my wrist told me it was 8:35, so I hadn't quite stretched it to the hour and ten minutes Wolfe had specified, but pretty close. He emerged from the door to the dining room, which is across the hall from the office, stood there while we filed in, and then followed, the look on his face as black as the coffee he had just been sipping. After crossing to his desk and lowering his overwhelming bulk into his chair, he growled at them, "Sit down, please."

They stayed on their feet. Aubry demanded, "What's the big idea? Goodwin says you have one."

"You will please sit down," Wolfe said coldly. "I look at people I'm talking to, especially when I suspect them of trying to flummox me, and my neck is not elastic."

His tone made it evident that what was biting him was nothing trivial. Caroline sidled to the red leather chair and sat on its edge. Aubry plopped on the yellow one and met Wolfe's level gaze.

"You suspect?" he asked quietly. "Who? Of What?"

"I think one of you has seen and talked with Mr. Karnow—today. Perhaps both of you."

"What makes you think so?"

"I reserve that. Whether and when I disclose it depends on you. While complete candor is too much to expect, it should at least be approximated when you're briefing a man for a job you want done. When and where did you see Mr. Karnow, and what was said?"

"I didn't. I have never him. I told you that. What's the idea of this?"

Wolfe's head moved. "Then it was you, madam?"

Caroline was staring at him, her brow creased.

"Are you suggesting that I saw my—that I saw Sidney Karnow today?"

"Precisely."

"Well, I didn't! I haven't seen him at all! And I want to know why you're suggesting that!"

"You will." Wolfe rested his elbows on the chair arms, leaned forward, and gave her his straightest and hardest look. She met it. He turned his head to the right and aimed the look at Aubry, and had it met again.

The doorbell rang.

Fritz was in the kitchen doing the dishes, so I got up and went to the hall and flipped the switch of the light out on the stoop and took a look through the one-way glass panel of the front door. What I saw deserved admiration. Sergeant Purley Stebbins of Manhattan Homicide West knew that that panel was one-way glass and he was visible, but he wasn't striking a pose; he just stood there, his big broad pan a foot away from the glass, to him opaque, a dick doing his duty.

I went and opened the door and spoke through the two-inch crack which was all the chain bolt would allow. "Hello there. It wasn't me, honest."

"Okay, comic." His deep bass was a little hoarse, as usual. "Then I won't take you. Let me in."

"For what?"

"I'll tell you. Do you expect me to talk through this damn crack?"

"Yes. If I let you in you'll tramp right over me to bust in on Mr. Wolfe, and he's in a bad humor. So am I. I can spare you ten seconds to loosen up. One, two, three, four—"

He cut me off. "You were just up at the Hotel Churchill. You left there about a half an hour ago with a man named Paul Aubry and his wife, and got into a taxi with them. Where are they? Did you bring them here?"

"May I call you Purley?" I asked.

"You goddam clown."

"All right, then, I won't. After all these years you should know better. Eighty-seven and four-tenths per cent of the people, including licensed detectives, who are asked impertinent questions by cops, answer quick because they are either scared or ignorant of their rights or anxious to cooperate. That lets me out. Give me one reason why I should tell you anything about my movements or any companions I may have had, and make it good."

Silence. After a moment I added, "And don't try to avoid giving me a shock. Since you're Homicide, some-one is dead. Who?"

"Who do you think?"

"Huh-uh. I won't try to guess because I might guess the right one and I'd be in the soup."

"I want to be around when you are. Sidney Karnow was killed in his room at the Churchill this afternoon. He had been reported dead in Korea and had just turned up alive, and had learned that his wife had mar-ried Paul Aubry. As if I was telling you anything you don't know."

He couldn't see my face through the crack, so I didn't have to bother about managing it. I asked, "Karnow was murdered?"

"That's the idea. He was shot in the back of the head."

"Are you saying I knew about it?"

"Not so far. But you knew about the situation, since you were there with Aubry and the woman. I want 'em, and I want 'em now, and are they here? If not, where are they?"

"I see," I said judiciously. "I admit you have given me a reason. Be seated while I go take a look." I pushed the door shut, went back to the office and crossed to my desk, took a pencil and my memo pad, and wrote:

Stebbins. Says K. murdered. We were seen leaving hotel. Asks are they here and if not where.

I got up to hand it to Wolfe, and he took it in with a glance and slipped it into the top drawer of his desk. He looked at Caroline and then at Aubry. "You don't need me," he told them. "Your problem has been solved for you. Mr. Karnow is dead."

They gawked at him.

"Of course," he added, "you now have another problem, which may be even thornier."

Caroline was stiff, frozen. "I don't believe it," Aubry said harshly.

"It seems authentic," Wolfe declared. "Archie?"

"Yes, sir. Sergeant Stebbins of Homicide is out on the stoop. He says that Karnow was murdered, shot in the back of the head, this afternoon in his room at the Churchill. Mr. Aubry and Mrs. Karnow were seen leaving the hotel with me, and he wants to know if they're here, and if not, where? He says he wants them."

"Good God," Aubry said. Caroline had let out a gasp, but no word. She was still rigid.

Her lips moved, and I thought she asked, "He's dead?" but it was too low to be sure.

Wolfe spoke. "So you have another problem. The police will give you a night of it, and possibly a week or a month. Mr. Stebbins cannot enter this house without a search warrant, and if you were my clients I wouldn't mind letting him wait on the stoop while we considered the matter, but since the job you gave me is now not feasible I am no longer in your hire. I have on occasion welcomed an opportunity to plague the police, but never merely for pastime, so I must bid you good evening."

Caroline had left her chair and gone to Aubry with her hands out, and he had taken them and pulled her to him. Evidently the ban was off.

"However," Wolfe continued, "I have a deep repugnance to letting the police take from my house people who have been moved to consult me and who have not been formally charged with a crime. There is a back way out, leading to Thirty-fourth Street, and Mr. Goodwin will take you by it if you feel that you would like a little time to discuss matters."

"No," Aubry said. "We have nothing to run from. Tell him we're here. Let him in."

Wolfe shook his head. "Not in my house, to drag you out. You're sure you don't want to delay it?"

"Yes."

"Then Archie, will you please handle it?"

I arose, told them, "This way, please," and headed for the door, but stopped and turned when I heard Caroline find her voice behind me.

"Wait a minute," she said, barely loud enough for me to get it. She was standing facing Aubry, gripping his lapels. "Paul, don't you think—shouldn't we ask Mr. Wolfe—"

"There's nothing to ask him." Aubry was up, with an arm across her shoulders. "I've had enough of Wolfe. Come on, Caro mia. We don't have to ask anybody anything."

They came and followed me into the hall. As Aubry

was getting his hat from the rack I opened the door, leaving the chain bolt on, and spoke to Purley. "What do you know, they were right here in the office. That's a break for you. Now if—"

"Open the door!"

"In a moment. Mr. Wolfe is peevish and might irritate you, so if you'll remove yourself, on down to the sidewalk, I'll let them out, and they are yours."

"I'm coming in."

"No. Don't even think of it."

"I want you too."

"Yeah, I thought so. I'll be along shortly. Twentieth Street?"

"Now. With me."

"Again no. I have to ask Mr. Wolfe if there's anything we wouldn't want to bother you with, and if so what. Where do I go, Twentieth Street?"

"Yes, and not tomorrow."

"Right. Glad to oblige. The subjects are here at my elbow, so if you'll just descend the steps—and be careful, don't fall."

He muttered something I didn't catch, turned, and started down. When he was at the bottom of the seven steps I removed the bolt, swung the door open, and told our former clients, "Okay. In return for the sandwiches and coffee, here's a suggestion. Don't answer a single damn question until you have got a lawyer and talked with him. Even if—"

I stopped because my audience was going. Aubry had her arm as they crossed the stoop and started down. Not wishing to give Purley the pleasure of having me watch him take them, I shut the door, replaced the bolt, and returned to the office. Wolfe was leaning back with his eyes closed.

"I'm wanted," I told him. "Do I go?"

"Of course," he growled.

"Are we saving anything?"

"No. There's nothing to save."

"The letters from Karnow to his wife are in my desk. Do I take them and turn them over?"

"No. They are her property, and doubtless she will claim them."

"Did I discover the body?"

"Certainly not. To what purpose?"

"None. Don't worry if I'm late."

I went to the hall for my hat and beat it.

III

Since I wasn't itching to oblige Homicide, and it was a pleasant evening for a walk, I decided to hoof it the fifteen blocks to Twentieth Street, and also to do a little chore on the way. If I had done it in the office Wolfe would have pulled his dignity on me and pretended to be outraged, though he knew as well as I did that it's always desirable to get your name in the paper, provided it's not in the obituary column. So I went to a phone booth in a drugstore on Tenth Avenue, dialed the *Gazette* number, asked for Lon Cohen, and got him.

"Scrap the front page," I told him, "and start over. If you don't want it I'll sell it to the *Times*. Did you happen to know that Paul Aubry and his wife, Mrs. Sidney Karnow to you, called on Nero Wolfe this afternoon, and I went somewhere with them, and brought them back to Mr. Wolfe's office, and fifteen minutes ago Sergeant Purley Stebbins came and got them? Or maybe you don't even know that Karnow was murd—"

"Yeah, I know that. What's the rest of it? Molasses you licked off your fingers?"

"Nope. Guaranteed straight as delivered. I just want to get my employer's name in the paper. Mine is spelled, A-R-C-H—"

"I know that too. Who else has got this?"

"From me, nobody. Only you, son."

"What did they want Wolfe to do?"

Of course that was to be expected. Give a newspaperman an inch and he wants a column. I finally convinced him that that was all for now and resumed my way downtown.

At Manhattan Homicide West on Twentieth Street I was hoping to be assigned to Lieutenant Rowcliff so I could try once more to make him mad enough to stutter, but I got a college graduate named Eisenstadt who presented no challenge. All he wanted was facts, and I dished them out, withholding, naturally, that I had entered the room. It took less than an hour, including having my statement typed and signed, and I declined his pressing invitation to stick around until Inspector Cramer got in. I told him another fact, that I was a citizen in good standing, or fair at least, with a known address, and could be found if and when needed.

Back at the office Wolfe was yawning at a book. The yawn was an act. He wanted to make it clear to me that losing a fee of five grand was nothing to get riled about. I had a choice: either proceed to rile him or go up to bed. They were equally attractive, and I flipped a quarter and caught it. He didn't ask me what I was deciding because he thought I wanted him to. It was heads, and I told him my session at Homicide wasn't worth reporting, said good night, and mounted the two flights to my room.

In the morning, at breakfast in the kitchen, with

Fritz supplying me with hot griddle cakes and the paper propped in front of me, I saw that I had given Lon not one inch but two. He had stretched it because it was exclusive. Aside from that, there was a pile of miscellaneous information, such as that Karnow had an Aunt Margaret named Mrs. Raymond Savage, and she had a son Richard, and a daughter Ann, now married to one Norman Horne. There was a picture of Ann, and also one of Caroline, not very good.

I seldom see Wolfe in the morning until eleven, when he comes down from the plant rooms, and that morning I didn't see him at all. A little after ten a call came from Sergeant Stebbins to invite me to drop in at the District Attorney's office at my earliest inconvenience. I don't apologize for taking only four minutes to put weights on papers on my desk, phone up to Wolfe, and get my hat and go, because there was a chance of running into our former clients, and they might possibly be coming to the conclusion that they hadn't had enough of Wolfe after all.

I needn't have been in such a hurry. In a large anteroom on an upper floor at 155 Leonard Street I sat for nearly half an hour on a hard wooden chair, waiting. I was about ready to go over to the window and tell the veteran female that another three minutes was all I could spare when another female appeared, coming from a corridor that led within. That one was not veteran at all, and I postponed my ultimatum. The way she moved was worthy of study, her face invited a full analysis, her clothes deserved a complete inventory, and either her name was Ann Savage Horne or the *Gazette* had run the wrong picture.

She saw me taking her in, and reciprocated frankly, her head tilted a little to one side, came and sat on a chair near mine, and gave me the kind of straight look that you expect only from a queen or a trollop.

I spoke. "What's that stole?" I asked her. "Rabbit?"

She smiled to dazzle me and darned near made it. "Where did you get the idea," she asked back, "that vulgarity is the best policy?"

"It's not policy; I was born vulgar. When I saw your picture in the paper I wondered what your voice was like, and I wanted to hear it. Talk some more."

"Oh. You're one up on me."

"I don't mind squaring it. I am called Goodwin, Archie Goodwin."

"Goodwin?" she frowned a little. She brightened. "Of course! You're in the paper too—if you're that one. You work for Nero Wolfe?"

"I practically *am* Nero Wolfe, when it comes to work. Where were you yesterday afternoon from eleven minutes past two until eighteen minutes to six?"

"Let's see. I was walking in the park with my pet flamingo. If you think that's no alibi, you're wrong. My flamingo can talk. Ask me some more."

"Can your flamingo tell time?"

"Certainly. It wears a wristwatch on its neck."

"How can it see it?"

She nodded. "I knew you'd ask that. It has been trained to tie its neck in a knot, just a plain single knot, and when it does that the watch is on a bend so that— well, Mother?" She was suddenly out of her chair and moving. "What, no handcuffs on anybody?"

Mother, Sidney Karnow's Aunt Margaret, leading a procession emerging from the corridor, would have made two of her daughter Ann and more than half of Nero Wolfe. She was large not only in bulk but also in facial detail, each and all of her features being so big

that space above her chin was at a premium. Besides
her was a thin young man, runty by comparison, wear-
ing black-rimmed glasses, and behind them were two
other males, one, obviously, from his resemblance to
Mother, Ann's brother Richard, and the other a tall
loose-jointed specimen who would have been called
distinguished-looking by any woman between sixteen
and sixty.

As I made my swift survey the flamingo trainer
was going on. "Mother, this is Mr. Goodwin—the Archie Goodwin who was at the Churchill yesterday with
Caroline and Paul. He's grilling me. Mr. Goodwin, my
mother, my brother Dick, my husband, Norman Horne
—no, not the one with the cheaters, that's Jim Beebe,
the lawyer to end all laws. *This* is my husband." The
distinguished-looking one had pushed by and was
beside her. She was flowing on. "You know how disap-
pointed I was at the District Attorney being so god-
awful polite to us, but Mr. Goodwin is different. He's
going to give me the third degree—physically, I mean;
he's built for it, and I expect I'll go to pieces and confess—"

Her husband's palm pressed over her mouth, firm
but not rough, stopped her. "You talk too much, darling," he said tolerantly.

"It's her sense of humor," Aunt Margaret ex-
plained. "All the same, Ann dear, it *is* out of place, with
poor Sidney just cruelly murdered. *Cruelly.*"

"Nuts," Dick Savage snapped.

"It *was* cruel," his mother insisted. "Murder *is*
cruel."

"Sure it was," he agreed, "but for us Sid has been
dead more than two years, and he's been alive again
only two weeks, and we never even saw him, so what
do you expect?"

"I suggest," Beebe the lawyer put in, in a high thin voice that fitted his stature perfectly, "that this is rather a public spot for a private discussion. Shall we go?"

"I can't," Ann declared. "Mr. Goodwin is going to wear me down and finally break me. Look at his hard gray eyes. Look at his jaw."

"Now, darling," Norman Horne said affectionately, and took her elbow and started her toward the door. The others filed after them, with Beebe in the rear. Not one mentioned the pleasure it had given them to meet me, though the lawyer did let me have a nod of farewell as he went by.

As I stood and watched the door closing behind them the veteran female's voice came. "Mr. Mandelbaum will see you, Mr. Goodwin."

Only two assistant district attorneys rate corner rooms, and Mandelbaum wasn't one of them. Halfway down the corridor, his door was standing open, and, entering, I had a surprise. Mandelbaum was at his desk, and across from him, on one of the two spare chairs that the little room sported, was a big husky guy with graying hair, a broad red face, and gray eyes that had been found hard to meet by tougher babies than Mrs. Norman Horne. If she called mine hard she should have seen those of Inspector Cramer of Homicide.

"I'm honored," I said appreciatively and accepted Mandelbaum's invitation to use the third chair.

"Look at me," Cramer commanded.

I did so with my brows up, which always annoys him.

"I'm late for an appointment," he said, "so I'll cut it short. I've just been up to see Wolfe. Of course he corroborates you, and he says he has no client. I've read your statement. I tell you frankly that we have no proof that you entered that hotel room."

"Now I can breathe again," I said with feeling.

"Yeah. The day you stop I'll eat as usual. I admit we have no proof, as yet, that you went in that room, but I know damn well you did. Information that the body was there came to us over the phone in a voice that was obviously disguised. You won't deny that I know pretty well by now how you react to situations."

"Sure. Boldly, bravely, and brilliantly."

"I only say I know. Leaving Aubry and Mrs. Karnow down in the bar, you go up and knock on the door of Karnow's room, and get no answer. In that situation there's not one chance in a thousand that you would leave without trying the knob."

"Then I must have."

"So you did?"

I stayed patient and reasonable. "Either I didn't try the knob—"

"Can it. Of course you did, and you found the door wasn't locked. So you opened it and called Karnow's name and got no answer, and you went in and saw the body. That I know, because I know you, and also because of what followed. You went back down to the bar and sat with them a while, and then took them back to Wolfe. Why? Because you knew Karnow had been murdered. If you had merely gone away when your knock wasn't answered, you would have stuck there until Karnow showed, if it took all night. And that's not half of it. When Stebbins went to Wolfe's place after them, with no warrant and no charge entered, Wolfe meekly handed them over! He says they were no longer his clients, since Stebbins had brought the news that Karnow was dead, but why weren't they? Because he won't take a murderer for a client knowingly, and he thought Aubry had killed Karnow. That's why."

I shook my head. "Gee, if you already know everything, I don't see why you bother with me."

"I want to know exactly what you did in that room, and whether you changed anything or took anything." Cramer leaned to me. "Look, Goodwin, I advise you to unload. The way it's going, I fully expect Aubry to break before the day's out, and when he does we'll have it all, including what you told them you had seen in Karnow's room when you rejoined them in the bar, and why the three of you went back to Wolfe's place. If you let me have it now I won't hold it against you that — What are you grinning for?"

"I'm thinking of Mr. Wolfe's face when I tell him this. When Stebbins came with the news that Karnow was dead, and therefore the job was up the flue, Mr. Wolfe hinted as far as his dignity would let him that he would consider another job if they had one, but they sidestepped it. So this will upset him. He keeps telling me we mustn't get discouraged, that some day you will be right about something, but this will be a blow—"

Cramer got up and tramped from the room.

I let Mandelbaum have the tail end of the grin. "Is he getting more sensitive?"

"Someday," the Assistant DA declared, "certain people are going to decide that Wolfe and you are doing more harm than good, and you won't have so much fun without a license. I'm too busy to play games. Please beat it."

When I got back to Thirty-fifth Street, a little after noon, Wolfe was at his desk, fiddling with stacks of cards from the files, plant germination records. I asked if he wanted a report of my visit with Mandelbaum and Cramer, and he said none was needed because he had talked with Cramer and knew the nature of his current befuddlement. I said I had met Karnow's relatives and also his lawyer, and would he care for my impressions, and got no reply but a rude grunt, so I passed it and went to my desk to finish some chores that had been interrupted by Stebbins' phone call. I had just started in when the doorbell rang, and I went to the hall to answer it.

Caroline Karnow was there on the stoop. I went and opened the door, and she stepped in.

"I want to see Mr. Wolfe," she blurted, and proved it by going right on, to the office door and in. I am supposed to block visitors until I learn if Wolfe will see them, but it would have taken a flying tackle, and I let her go and merely followed. By the time I got there she was in the red leather chair as if she owned it.

Wolfe, a germination card in each hand, was scowling at her.

"They've arrested him," she said. "For murder."

"Naturally," Wolfe growled.

"But he didn't do it!"

"Also naturally. I mean naturally you would say that."

"But it's true! I want you to prove it."

Wolfe shook his head. "Not required. They must prove he did. You're all tight, madam. Too tight. Have you eaten today?"

"Good lord," she said, "all you two think about is eating. Last night him, and now—" She started to laugh, at first a sort of gurgle, and then really out with it. I got up and went to her, took her head between my hands to turn her face up, and kissed her on the lips unmistakably. With some customers that is more satisfactory than a slap, and just as effective. I paid no attention to her first convulsive jerks, and released her head only when she quit shaking and got hold of my hair. I pulled loose and backed up a step.

"What on earth—" She gasped.

I decided she had snapped out of it, went to the kitchen and asked Fritz to bring crackers and milk and hot coffee, and returned. As I sat at my desk she demanded, "Did you have to do that?"

"Look," I said, "evidently you came to get Mr. Wolfe to help you. He can't stand hysterical women, and in another four seconds he would have been out of the room and would have refused to see you again. That's one angle of it. I am going on talking to give both you and Mr. Wolfe a chance to calm down. Another angle is that if you think it's undesirable to be kissed by me I am willing to submit it to a vote by people who ought to know."

She was passing her hands over her hair. "I suppose I should thank you?"

"You're welcome."

"Are you recovered," Wolfe rasped, "or not?"

"I'm all right." She swallowed. "I haven't slept, and it's quite true I haven't eaten anything, but I'm all right. They've arrested Paul for murder. He wants me to get a lawyer, and of course I have to, but I don't know who. The one he uses in business is no good for this, and certainly Jim Beebe won't do, and two other lawyers I know—I don't think they're much good. I told Paul I was coming to you, and he said all right."

"You want me to recommend a lawyer?"

"Yes, but we want you too. We want you to do— well, whatever you do." Suddenly she was flushing, and the color was good for her face. "Paul says you charge very high, but I suppose I have lots of money again, now that Sidney is dead." The flush deepened. "I've got to tell you something. Last night when you told us about it, that Sidney had been murdered, for just one second I thought Paul had done it—one awful second."

"I know you did. Only I would say ten seconds. Then you went to him."

"Yes. I went and touched him and let him touch me, and then it was over, but it was horrible. And that's partly why I must ask you, do you believe Paul killed him?"

"No," Wolfe said flatly.

"You're not just saying that?"

"I never just say anything." Wolfe suddenly realized that he had swiveled his chair away from her when she started to erupt, and now swung it back. "Mr. Cramer, a policeman, came this morning and twitted me for having let a murderer hoodwink me. When he had gone I considered the matter. It would have to be that Mr. Aubry, having killed Mr. Karnow, and having discussed it with you, decided to come and engage me to deal with Karnow in order to establish the fact that he didn't know Karnow was dead. That is Mr. Cramer's position, and I reject it. I sat here for an hour yesterday, listening to Mr. Aubry and looking at him, and if he had just come from killing the man he was asking me to deal with, I am a dolt. Since I am not a dolt, Mr. Aubry is not a murderer. Therefore—Yes, Fritz. Here's something for you, madam."

I would like to think it was my kiss that gave her an appetite, but I suppose it was the assurance from Wolfe that he didn't think her Paul was guilty of murder. She disposed not only of the crackers and milk but also of a healthy portion of toast spread with Fritz's liver pâté and chives, while Wolfe busied himself with the cards and I found something to do on my desk.